Promise
of
Mars

Promise

_of_

Mars

Arc True

Promise of Mars

Printed in the United States of America

ISBN: 9798517039200

To my wife, Sara.

CONTENTS

ACKNOWLEDGMENTS

I would like to thank Isabel Pettibone, Kaz Morran, Ana Hantt, and Josie Baron, for all they did for this book.

CHAPTER 1: GREENHOUSES

Consider using LEDs to light a one-acre farm on Mars. Good solar panels have an efficiency of 22 percent, and great LEDs have an efficiency of 35 percent. With Mars' solar irradiance of 59 percent, you would need a minimum of 22 acres of solar panels for the plants to receive the same amount of light as on Earth.

For a small outpost, that is doable. But to feed Promise's population of 304,667, you would need 2,500 acres of greenhouse, which in turn would require you to build 55,000 acres of solar panels. That's 86 square miles, or a twentieth of all solar panels ever made. And that's for the lights alone. Luckily, no one farmed that way on Mars.

Having finished my count, I moved my hand down from where it blocked the sun's glare. I wrote "174 wheat plants per meter" in the top left corner of my notebook. Hmm. Well within normal. No decaying plant matter; no smell of rot. None of the cracks in the concrete floor had more than a two-millimeter gap. Where was all the oxygen going?

I was an accountant with the Mars Accountants and Resource Society. I was also confused. Greenhouse 211 produced less oxygen than the math said it should. In fact, it produced the least of all 309 greenhouses.

Oxygen accounting for a greenhouse is harder than for other facilities. Plants are unpredictable, and their oxygen production varies day to day. But in the end, a certain weight of product should equate to a certain weight of oxygen.

I walked over to a farmer filling a crack in the cement floor with rubber sealant. Greenhouses are softsuit areas, so it took a gentle prod to get his attention.

I asked, "Any trouble with the cracks lately?"

He straightened up and turned to squarely face me.

"I'm not hiding anything from MARS."

Somewhat disgruntled that he could tell I worked for the Mars Accountants and Resource Society, I said, "I'm not making any accusations. I'm just looking to do my accounting."

"That's probably what you told the foreman over at Greenhouse 19."

He was referring to a case two years ago involving a

foreman with a three-millimeter crack in the floor of his greenhouse. The floors were made from alternating layers of rubber sealant and cement. As long as the cracks were small enough, the rubber would stretch and still hold a seal.

The foreman at Greenhouse 19 hadn't wanted to dig a trench all 350 feet across his concrete floor to fix the crack. Instead, his workers filled it in with rubber the same way small cracks were repaired. They then hid it with cement. The crack caused a 2 percent leak in the oxygen seal. It was so well hidden that it took my coworker, Ryan Decker, a full four weeks to track it down.

I said, "We wouldn't have cared about the leak if he hadn't fudged his production numbers to cover it up. His boss may have cared, but at MARS, we only record where the oxygen goes. We don't make judgments about it."

Stooping to unclip a sheet of reflective Mylar from its post and gently fold it off to the side, the farmer ran his thumb along the crack.

"How many millimeters?" I asked.

"1.1" He looked up, expecting me to argue with his measuring method. I had measured enough concrete cracks in my five years as an accountant on Mars not to doubt him. My current accuracy was within 0.2 millimeters, but he did this far more than I did.

3

"Thank you," I said, writing the measurement down in my notepad. That seemed to satisfy him.

Coming to the four-foot-wide row of grain, the farmer lifted a section of the grow tray that was filled with soil and wheat and set it off to the side. On Earth, it would have been over 130 pounds; here on Mars, it weighed only fifty.

Continuing with the rubber sealant, he filled the crack until he came to the next row of Mylar reflectors. The whole greenhouse was laid out like this. It alternated four feet of reflectors, four feet of wheat, another four feet of reflectors, and then a two-foot walking path.

I decided to ask him a question; people always seemed happy to explain to an outsider why they were stupid.

"I always wonder why the greenhouses are laid out in such long rows. It's 3,200 feet by 350 feet. That's rather long and skinny. Wouldn't it be better just to build them more square?"

"Geometry."

Not really an answer. I waited until he came to the conclusion he needed to tell me more.

"The problem with solar reflectors," he said as he waved his hand at the 3,200-foot-long row of four-foot-wide shiny foil, "is that the sun moves throughout the day, and it would take heavy, complicated machinery to keep a reflector pointed at the same spot in the field all day. As you can see here, there is nothing complicated about our reflectors. Just Mylar rectangles held at the correct angle by posts in the corners. A combination of the greenhouses running east to west and the reflectors being directly next to the wheat means most of the light hitting the reflectors hits the wheat. Works out to each plant getting a little over double the sunlight it otherwise would on Mars. Brings the light level up to about 1.1 of Earth-normal."

"What about the plants at the ends?" I asked.

"They don't receive as much light. That's why the greenhouses are so long. It's so there are fewer ends. We plant leafy greens there since they are more tolerant of low-light levels."

I said, "So, you never have to move the reflectors?" This seemed unlikely, as the only thing farmers ever seemed to do was move reflectors.

"On a daily basis, no, but over the course of a year, the sun changes its angle in the sky by over fifty degrees. Every four weeks, we have to come through and change the angle on the reflectors. You can get away with eight to ten weeks, but yields suffer a little."

Now, for a question I knew the answer to. "All these reflectors—did they take a lot of weight to ship from Earth?"

"Hardly. One ton of Mylar could cover an entire five acres." Martians liked numbers. Almost no one came here who didn't know calculus and a little physics.

Now, time for a little prying. "I've seen a lot of people work with rubber, and that's some solid work you're doing. I bet you're better at it than anyone else around here."

Ruining my follow-up question, he said, "Neither better nor worse, given I'm the only one who works on the seals."

So much for an easy win by repeating Decker's findings. This farmer was doing a great job. If no one else repaired the cracks, I doubted a leaky greenhouse would account for the missing oxygen.

Continuing down the path, I smiled at the earthy aroma. Of all the colony, this felt the most like home. Standing in the sun with my eyes closed, I waved my hand through the wheat and imagined I was on my cousin's farm in Ohio.

Focusing back on my assignment, I approached another farmer adjusting reflectors.

"Can I have a moment of your time?" I asked.

"What do you need? This is a high radiation area, and I don't want to be stuck out here long."

He was right. The thin glass ceiling provided much less radiation protection than anywhere else in the colony. The wheat didn't mind much. Even Earth strains are forty times more radiation-resistant than humans, and natural selection had worked fast with such a strong forcing function. The farmers only came out into the fields to make repairs and move reflectors. All the hydroponics, planting, and harvesting was automated.

He adjusted the Mylar one notch down. No wrinkles. No misalignment. Nothing to reduce photosynthesis or oxygen production.

"I'm Jack Maddox, an accountant with MARS," I said.

Dusting off his well-worn uniform, he said, "I could tell you were with MARS by the clean softsuit. What do you need?"

A half-torn-off nametag read John Saville.

"Your oxygen farm here produces the least oxygen of any greenhouse." A more direct route this time.

"Oxygen farm? We mostly grow wheat," he said.

"You can't starve to death on Mars," I said.

"Why's that?" he asked. "Seems simple enough to me. We just stop planting wheat, and then later, we would all starve."

I closed my notebook and said, "No, you would suffocate long before. We receive no food or oxygen shipments from Earth. When wheat makes one kilogram of grain, it also makes 0.2 kilograms of oxygen. When you later eat the grain, you burn 0.2 kilograms of oxygen. It makes a nearly perfect circle."

He walked to a reflector and began to adjust it. "You're forgetting about the part of the plant that's not grain."

I said, "There are some side notes like the carbon in chaff

and poop, but since that is all fed into the bioreactors, it all breaks down in the end."

A loud *puuuffffft* temporarily stopped the conversation. A service vehicle was equalizing pressure with the farm.

I continued, "The problem is all our buildings leak. While it's only about one percent per year, that's still over fifteen hundred tons of oxygen. The longer time passes, the more oxygen debt we build up. After ten years, we have lost well over fifteen thousand tons of oxygen."

"So?"

I said, "That means, somewhere in the colony, there are seventy-five thousand tons of grain we could never eat since we've lost the oxygen to go with it. By the time you ate all the other food in the colony and tried to start on the remaining seventy-five thousand tons, you would be out of oxygen. That's why it is impossible for the colony to starve. We would all suffocate first."

Having finished adjusting the reflector, he moved on to the next one. "What about oxygenators? None of the early Mars missions had plants. They just converted CO_2 to O_2."

I followed him to the next reflector and said, "MOXIE was the first oxygenator on Mars. It took twenty-five kilowatt-hours per day to make enough oxygen for one person. The technology has improved since then, but even so, oxygenators require a lot of power to operate. Only boutique locations have them. If all the oxygenators on Mars ran at full capacity, they would only supply enough oxygen for about a thousand people."

"Still, we grow wheat, and people eat wheat. This is a wheat farm," he said.

"As you wish. Any idea where your oxygen is going?"

"No."

"Your farm is the lowest producer of oxygen," I said, opening my notebook to the appropriate page.

"Somebody has to be. That's the way numbers work."

Great, he was explaining numbers to an accountant.

Puuufffft again.

I said, "Your wheat yields are in the bottom quartile but not at the very bottom. You're making the oxygen. It's just going somewhere."

"Maybe it's the harvesters. A few of them have jumped their tracks in the last year."

"How would that affect the oxygen?" I closed my notebook and put it in my pocket.

"I don't know. That's not my thing," said the farmer.

Puuufffft.

"Okay, I'll keep looking around," I said.

The truth was I had already found the source of the oxygen

anomaly. It had become apparent during the conversation. The service vehicles had made the *puuufffft* sound of inrushing air when they docked, not the *poooffft* sound of outflowing air. A casual observer would likely have missed the difference, but I had spent five years following the flow of air in great detail.

The greenhouses were a low-pressure area in the colony. Due to the limited radiation shielding from the thin glass ceiling, everyone had to wear softsuits. With everyone in softsuits, there was no reason to keep the air pressure above what the plants needed. The pressure in the cabin of the service vehicle should not have been lower than the greenhouse's.

I had found a pretty good scam. A technician working in a local garage could steal the oxygen in the cabin of an automated service vehicle by pumping it out once sealed.

The next time it docked with a greenhouse, the pressures would equalize, hiding his crime. Greenhouse oxygen levels are so variable and the amount of oxygen stolen so small, no one had noticed.

Proceeding to walk around the farm, I made a show of inspecting seals and counting plants. It was unlikely any of the farmers were in on the scam, but it pays to be careful. Absentmindedly, I walked over to an airlock and waited for the next service vehicle to arrive.

A small hanging basket with daisies bloomed next to a

cement column. Their yellow centers and white petals stood out in stark contrast to the red dust outside—vibrant life in this barren world. I checked my helmet's faceplate. In an emergency, it would flip down and seal the suit.

Poooffft.

That was outflowing air, so not all the vehicles were involved. I continued to amble down the walkway, stopping to count wheat plants in front of another airlock.

Puuuffft.

The slight breeze blowing past my face confirmed the air was moving into the service vehicle.

Finishing my count, I left the greenhouse, making sure to pass the daisies on the way out. The report would get filed once I returned to the office. It would be up to Bruce to find the culprits after that.

Bruce Trummer was the FBI agent assigned to resource theft. I counted where the oxygen went but didn't have an opinion on who it belonged to. Bruce, on the other hand, had strong opinions about that.

CHAPTER 2: TACOS

Promise was the third attempt to build a Martian colony. Much of its design oriented around avoiding the reasons the second colony, Plymouth, had failed. A large US aerospace corporation had founded Plymouth as a railroad-style land grab. After a year, its population had grown to only thirty of the planned two thousand, but progress was being made. Buildings were being constructed, farms planted, and mines surveyed. But on Earth, the company was becoming less and less profitable with the possibility of bankruptcy. The colonists became nervous about being stranded on Mars.

The company had already deployed a year's worth of food, water, and shelter for two thousand people. They gifted it to the thirty colonists, hoping a lifetime of resources would placate them.

Unfortunately, the company had miscalculated their employees' fear. All thirty colonists canceled their contracts and returned to Earth. They hadn't worried about starvation, or suffocation. They had worried about having to stay in cramped underground bunkers for the rest of their lives. Who in their right mind would choose to stay there?

Stepping off the transit line, I saw my housing unit from a hundred meters away. The blocky, four-story building sat among many similar structures. The brightly painted Martian concrete and Earth fixtures marked it as being in the "Early local" style. I tapped my fob on the door to the tunnel. As the door opened, I was charged £0.10 for air.

My shoulders relaxed as I entered the tunnel. The relief came from the added distance to the near-vacuum on the surface.

When I finished walking through the tunnel to my building, I used the fob again. No charge this time. This was home.

It was also where I worked. In the entryway, I headed to the reception desk to my left instead of to the residential elevator on my right.

"Jane," I said with a childish grin, "can you tell Darnell I accounted for my oxygen anomaly and that he will likely want to loop Bruce in for this one?"

"Already?" Her dark curls bounced as she said, "Ryan is going to throw a fit when he finds out. He had bet a hundred pounds you were going to take longer to solve a greenhouse anomaly than he did."

"Then I guess whoever won the bet can buy the first round of drinks."

Rolling her eyes, she said, "You know I don't go out with you guys when you celebrate. But since I won money because of you, I'd come if you asked."

"No need for that," I said. I enjoyed knowing my coworker would bet on me over Ryan. Though I would have preferred her to think I was attractive instead of smart.

I strolled to my desk, where my papers, computer, and pencils were all lined up in a neat row. Booting up the computer, I glanced at the photos of early oxygen tanks I had thumbtacked to the cubical wall. Engineers really had designed some clever canisters over the years.

Looking over my shoulder, I saw Ryan's empty desk. Rubbing in my success would have to wait.

The sun had begun to set, dimming the light coming through the windows that circled the upper two feet of the wall. The rest of the room was sunk below ground level, making this a zero-radiation area.

My manager, Darnell, sent me a text message: "Jack, I'm in a meeting. We will have to talk tomorrow. Make sure to send a copy of your report to Bruce if you think he would be interested."

I'd have just enough time to finish my report and then run

downstairs to my room and shower before everyone else would be ready to go out to celebrate.

The oxygen losses at Greenhouse 211 only amounted to a hundredth of a ton per week, but we would celebrate more for finding the leak than for the hundred thousand tons of O2 we had already accounted for. I guess we felt strongly about our books being accurate.

It was a beautiful report with complete calculations of oxygen stolen per vehicle, taking into account internal volumes, temperature, and frequency of docking. The oxygen ledger was updated to reflect the missing oxygen being relocated to Divio's Garage. I had found which garage based on service schedules.

Not only had oxygen been stolen from the greenhouse, the greenhouse had paid for air that should have flowed into it from the service vehicle. Bruce would be interested in all of this.

After forwarding the report to Darnell and Bruce, I got ready to go out. Halfway to the transit station, Bruce called.

"Jack, don't go talking about this report at Mahoney's tonight. This will be a simple case, and I'll easily round up everyone involved, but I still need two days before you go letting them know we're onto them."

How did he manage to swagger over the phone?

I said, "You know I'm discrete."

"I know you're going to retell the story in this report six times before the night is over. I would advise you to be aware of your surroundings, but with you, that's useless. Just don't sit next to any mechanics or farmers."

He had such a low opinion of my ability to keep a secret. As I proceeded to the transit station, I wondered if Ryan ever got these calls.

Mahoney's Irish Pub occupied the entire top floor of a nearby apartment building. It kept its low radiation certificate despite its floor-to-ceiling windows.

It did this mainly with a two-foot-thick concrete roof that jutted out in a ten-foot overhang. On Mars, the vast majority of radiation comes from above your head. Any radiation coming from the horizon has to go through fifty times more atmosphere. Mars has a thin atmosphere but not that thin.

For radiation protection, Mahoney's also had the local geography going for it. Promise is built in a valley with steep sides. This blocked all the radiation from the north and south.

The corner of the building pointed due east. This gave the inch-thick windows an effective 1.4 inches of thickness for the trickle of radiation from the east and west that made it through the fifty Mars atmospheres from the horizon. The views were spectacular.

By the time I walked off the elevator and paid the £0.10 oxygen fee, my coworkers had already arrived.

Ryan happily chatted with a woman I had never seen before. The other twelve accountants from the oxygen department milled around the door. Jamie and Benny were also there. They were with the water department, but that department was so small they normally came out with us.

Darnell wouldn't be coming. He was a manager and considered two beers to be wild drinking. Most of us wouldn't go that far, but Craig and Susan had been known to drink a full three beers in one sitting.

All the tables and most of the seats at the bar had already been taken.

Craig walked up to me and said, "Do the thing."

I pretended not to understand.

He said, "You know what I'm talking about. That group right over there would be perfect."

He gestured at what appeared to be nine or ten female programmers, who had clearly come together and been there for several hours.

"I don't see the point," I said. My coworkers had a strong belief that any woman I sat next to would leave within ten minutes.

Lately, they had been putting this to the test, and empirical evidence showed the time to be closer to sixty seconds. I thought the joke was in poor taste. My conversation skills were completely adequate. It's just that they would have me sit next to women who were finished with their evening. Of course they didn't stay long if they were already leaving.

Putting on a happy face, I sat in the open chair at the edge of the group. I asked the dark brunette next to me, "What do you think about those news reports of colonists who work in the mansions but are never seen in Promise? Do you think the government should enforce welfare visits to make sure they aren't being trafficked?"

She held up a finger and said, "I was just leaving."

She did, taking two of her friends with her.

The woman four seats away saw me looking at her. "Ah, did Margaret leave? I'd better catch up with her."

She pulled on a couple of her friends' arms, and they headed to the door in a bunch. I'm not sure what happened to the old lady and her companions to my left, but it didn't matter, as my friends moved in to take the available seats.

Ryan left the group he had been entertaining with some story that required him to wave his arms in large circles and sat next to me. He wore his typical flannel shirt and exercise pants.

He said, "Congratulations on solving your oxygen anomaly.

You sure made my four weeks look sad. Though, next time, I'll beat your new record."

"Good luck with that. Jane says she won a hundred pounds from you."

"The anomaly you were chasing was so small I thought it didn't even exist. I figured you were in for a yearlong goose chase."

"It was only a little at a time, but over the months, the numbers for the greenhouse had just kept drifting. I only noticed because the greenhouse already produced so little," I said.

We had strict rules about shoptalk when we were out. What counted as shoptalk was any number with more than two significant digits or complaints about how sloppily someone had filled out a Form 1077B. Everything else was okay.

Looking at the menu, I saw the chicken tacos were £1.23.

"At these prices, I could ship myself a chicken."

Ryan said, "Enjoy your taco and try to relax. It's always cheaper to eat at home, and you're not paying today. "

"True," I said.

All goods in Promise were priced in pounds. Not the funny British kind but the price of shipping one pound from Earth to Mars. And a £ was not the theoretical price either; it was a pre-purchased contract backed by both the freight company and a collection of insurance brokers. At current freight prices, the conversion rate was £1 = $50.

This system wasn't original to Promise; it had been predicted by the great authors of the twenty-first century. It allowed freight companies to be paid now for rockets they would build in the future. They could invest the enormous amount of funds required to build a slightly more efficient rocket, knowing they had already sold its entire lifetime of capacity. This led to steadily decreasing shipping prices.

We finished ordering our food and watched the lights of Promise twinkle. Beyond them, dark emptiness spread all the way to the horizon, where the stars started.

Ryan saw Benny walking between tables and waved him over to us.

Benny said, "I love that view. You can see the progress we've made in bringing life to this dead place. Before we came here, it was all dull, red dust. Now there are friends, music, and laughter in an ever-expanding bubble."

"I came thirty-eight million miles to be a part of that," Ryan said. He paused and took a drink of his beer before continuing, "People in my family thought I should have focused on Earth and its problems, but this feels like history and purpose."

"Your family were two steps behind in their thinking. The

problem with Earth is the people. If you leave two humans alone in a room long enough, they will start to fight," Benny said.

"That seems a little pessimistic. I get along with most people," Ryan said.

"You're not married. Ask anyone who has been. Jamie and I are happy, but we have as much conflict as anyone. On a larger societal scale, this is Earth's central problem."

"What does that have to do with Mars?" I asked.

"Conflict and tribalism go hand in hand. Groups in contact will start a conflict, just like a married couple. Once the conflict starts, its natural progression is an escalation until one side is destroyed. Facing an outside force together can prevent that. Either an enemy they can annihilate together or an epic project. Mars is that project."

"So, you don't think Mars is a distraction from Earth's problems? It's the solution?" I asked.

"Exactly. The human race has to feel like it is confronting something in order to progress. People need uplifting. There has to be a purpose beyond the bottom of a bottle," Benny said.

"In a marriage, people can stop their conflicts without having to face an outside obstacle," I said.

"True. But they only do that by becoming better people. Societies can also become better, but I'm not Martin Luther

King. That work is for someone else. I will build a colony in the wastes of Mars and push the boundaries of civilization."

Jamie came up and said, "Is my husband getting grandiose again? He'll try to convince you that famine on Earth will be solved by us dancing tango on Mars."

Benny said, "I told you before, every famine in the last thirty years has been caused by armed forces not letting food aid into the country. There are no problems on Earth anymore that aren't caused by groups fighting each other."

"How did conflict cause my mother to get cancer?" Jamie asked.

Benny quickly excused himself and went to buy a drink. I think he didn't like that line of questioning.

I turned to Jamie and said, "Is your answer any better? Why are you here?"

"You know perfectly well what my answer is. You've heard it many times before. For people like me, it's just what we do. There is a beauty to this that is hard to explain. You might as well ask an eagle why it flies," she said.

Craig walked past our group, so Ryan waved him over and said, "Jamie finally found a good answer to her husband's grand talk of Mars. Tell us again your odd reason for being here."

Craig said, "You've heard this before. I once met a PhD

who did research on an esoteric area of alligator physiology. I asked him why he devoted his life to studying such a random nook of science. He said because no one else was researching it. If any advancement happened in the field, it would be because of him."

Ryan said, "I still don't get how that led you to Mars."

He said, "Earth is too crowded. For any activity there you could imagine, there are already thousands of people doing it. Only the top quarter of a percent have any chance of making a mark. On Mars, everything is special and new. It is easy to be the first or best at something."

Ryan looked at me and said, "Jack, at least his reason is better than yours."

I said, "Hey, the retirement account for this job is phenomenal."

For the rest of the night, everyone had a good time, especially me, since I didn't have to pay. Afterwards, I stumbled home, laughing with Ryan at a joke involving a banana being self-depreciating but not self-deprecating. It wasn't that funny of a joke, but a beer and a half made everything funnier.

The door opened as I approached my bedroom. Like most Martians, I slept in the basement of the building I worked in. My bedside table was made of thin steel sheets. It was the second-cheapest material on Mars, and I didn't want cement furniture.

Ritualistically, I touched the no-radiation plaque on the wall, then fell into bed.

CHAPTER 3: THE FORGE

Farmers thought the greenhouses were the core of the colony. They made all the food and oxygen needed. In a real emergency, the whole population could crawl into the greenhouses and close the doors. Even with only enough power to keep the heat pumps running, everyone would be fine. There would be unlimited food and air.

But the real core of the colony was the Forge. Ninety-five percent of all non-rock objects on Mars had been made in the Forge. The cement for all the brightly painted buildings? Made in the Forge. The ubiquitous steel of every tool and vehicle? Made in the Forge. The beautifully clear glass that covered miles of greenhouses? Made in the Forge.

Today was an audit day. I spent most days at my desk, processing forms and updating the ledger, but on audit days, I got to explore Mars. The paperwork companies filed contained innumerable facts. We had to go out and make sure those facts were actually true. Some audits were triggered by problems with the numbers, like the case last week with the greenhouse. But most checks were quick and random.

The random number generator had picked three oxygen tanks for me. They were owned by Bob's Cement LLC, which, like most industrial companies, was in the Forge.

As we left the office, Jane stood up from her receptionist's desk, making her curls bounce. She said, "If you're going to be out late, I could get takeout for you. I was going to get some myself and don't like using the transit line when it's busy. I'm not planning on eating until after rush hour."

I said, "No, thank you. There is some food in my room."

"Are you sure? I'd love to hear about other parts of Mars. Most of the interesting places are privately owned, and I can't see them the same way you can."

"You want stories? I'll tell Susan, she always has some to tell."

The transit line took me west to the edge of the residential section of the city. There, the valley walls were shorter and widened out into an old impact crater. The brightly shining towers that dotted the area reminded me to pull down the sun visor on my hardsuit.

The Forge was a massive solar reflector array. Each

reflector was a two-hundred-by-one-hundred-foot shiny rectangle sitting on a dual-axis tracking post. A rim of thin steel held the silvered Mylar taut like a tent wall.

The United States uses about ninety thousand kilowatt-hours per person per year. For Mars to have the same per-capita energy use, the Forge would have needed eighteen square miles of reflectors. It had twenty-eight square miles. Mars was a tough place to live.

I found the crawler belonging to Bob's Cement and climbed aboard. The hardsuit made it an awkward walk up the ramp into the crawler.

As it drove out into the rows of reflectors, my hand kept going to my helmet latches. Two seals between me and the surface. My hardsuit and the wall of the crawler.

Dust filled the early-morning air as patches of reflectors performed their weekly cleaning routine. The reflectors tilted forward, pointing at the ground. Then, a metal object that looked like a fly swatter hit them like a drum. It was attached to a small capacitor that had been charging for the last several days. When it hit the taunt Mylar, it switched the Mylar's charge. The combination of mechanical and electrical forces efficiently knocked the dust off the reflectors and onto the crawler.

Our destination was one of the towers that was outshining

the sun. The Forge produced a bewildering 24.3 gigawatts of heat at peak capacity. That's giga, with a g. The heat was sold to owners of the fifty or sixty towers that dotted the crater. Most industrial processes need heat more than electricity, and by skipping the electricity step, the Forge was much more efficient than solar cells.

The driver wore a Bob's Cement name tag that indicated he was an engineer.

I said to the driver, "This solar field is bigger than anything I ever saw on Earth."

He was wearing a hardsuit but had taken his gloves and helmet off. "It is. If I remember correctly, it's about twenty times larger than any Earth installation. There are not a lot of other options for power on Mars, and it's actually easier to build these on Mars than Earth."

"Easier on Mars? You don't hear that about many things," I said.

"Seriously. The wind on Mars is much weaker, allowing the reflectors to be larger. The only weather we get is dust, and that is taken care of by the dust mitigation systems," he said.

"The fly swatters?"

"Yes."

We drove in silence for a while.

I said, "A farmer was telling me Mylar is cheap to ship."

"It really is. The entire reflective surface of the Forge only weighs six thousand six hundred tons. That's only sixty-six shiploads. Of course, the structural and control components of the reflectors weigh more, but overall they are still very light."

We drove in silence some more.

"Wait! That's a JPL-390!" I yelled while pointing.

One industry that had not made its way to Mars was waste management. There was so much empty land; companies just left trash where it fell. As the center of industrial production, the Forge was littered with piles of old equipment and products.

What I had spotted was an antique. When the early manned missions came to Mars, they brought enormous tanks of backup oxygen. The JPL-390 was one of the original tank designs. It could store a hundred tons of O2 and took up the entire cargo hold of an early Earth-to-Mars freighter. It was a lifetime supply of oxygen for three people.

I had never seen one before. They were replaced by newer models well before Promise had been founded.

"Let's go see that." I was enthusiastically waving in its direction.

"See what? All I see is trash," he said.

"That's a JPL-390. They're antiques. Haven't you wanted to see one?"

"I have no idea what you are talking about," he said, reluctantly slowing the crawler.

"It has to have been on Mars longer than the city of Promise."

"I don't care if it's been on Mars longer than Crazy Simeon Post," he said.

Simeon Post was a Syrian researcher who, fifty years ago, refused to leave Mars after his mission drilling rock cores along the Cerberus Fossae ended. He had said goodbye to the rest of his crew and traveled to the remains of Plymouth. He lived off the leftover emergency supplies, and once a year, he would radio Earth a list of the things he had "borrowed." Otherwise, he kept his radio off.

My conversation with the driver continued for a few more minutes. I wanted to go see the antique. He seemed uninterested and didn't want to make the detour. I had a distinct advantage in the discussion. The whole point of this trip was for me to inspect oxygen tanks. This one wasn't on the list, but he had been told to take me to the oxygen tanks I requested.

Standing in front of the tank, I was enthralled. I didn't even think about the thinness of my helmet faceplate. These old tanks were classics. They had no built-in gauges—just half a dozen valves. Its stainless steel shone silver in the sunlight.

The only part that was not cylindrical was at the top, where it tapered like the nosecone of a rocket.

Out of habit, I placed my gloved left hand on the tank and smacked it with my right. To my complete shock, it had the low pitch tremor of a full tank.

This tank had probably been sitting out here for forty years. Maybe it had been deployed in the first batch of supplies when Promise was founded. I doubted anyone knew it was still functioning and full. It definitely wasn't in the oxygen ledger.

Thirty minutes later, when the driver convinced me to get back in the crawler, we proceeded towards Bob's Cement.

He said, "Why do we have to let you come on our property at all? You're not part of the government."

"You don't have to let us come, but MARS has a contract with the city to maintain the resource ledgers. If we couldn't confirm your reports, then we would list your company as out of compliance with the Emergency Response Fund Creation Bill," I said.

"And that's bad?" he said.

I leaned back into my seat and relaxed. This was a common conversation for me. "Yes, very. About twenty years ago, the planning council calculated that if a disease wiped out all our crops and the first cargo ship from Earth didn't solve the problem, half the population would die waiting for the second.

So they passed a bill that taxes companies whose emergency resources are insufficient."

"So we let you come audit our company to avoid the tax?"

"Yes. The critical detail in the bill is that the amount collected every year is always the same. It is evenly split between all the companies paying the tax. So, as more and more companies complied, the tax per company went up and up. That created more and more incentive to have enough resources to avoid the tax. For the last five years, all companies on Mars have been in compliance. If a company became non-compliant, the two-million-pound tax would cripple it."

His eyebrow raised at hearing the size of the fine.

"That's a lot of money, but can't you schedule these audits farther out and at more convenient times? We are short-staffed due to moving our production to a new area in the quarry."

"Margret Lance is the CEO of MARS, and she does not tolerate interference in audits. If you deny us access, she won't care if later you show her enough oxygen to meet your reserve requirement. She will report to the government 'total resources available is unknown. Accounting in progress.' It will be technically true. She does not allow the ledger to include any approximate numbers."

When we pulled up to the cement factory, the driver led me to the three oxygen tanks on my list. I confirmed their oxygen levels and then was escorted to the office of the president of the company. I knew I would wait ten minutes. Enough time that I would know I was unimportant but not so much time that Mrs. Lance would feel she had been told the same.

"Jack Maddox, you can go in now," his secretary said.

Robert Soto sat behind his desk with gray hair and a simple smile. I knew there would be two minutes of polite conversation followed by the only question he cared about. Was he about to face a two-million-pound fine?

"So good to see you. Have a seat," he said.

"Thank you," I said.

"I take it your trip here was uneventful."

My eyes lit up as I remembered the JPL-390.

I said, "Actually, I found an enormous amount of oxygen out in the junk piles between the reflectors."

His face instantly paled. He choked out, "Found?" He was clearly trying to say more but failed.

I tried to recover the situation, "Not on Bob's Cement's property. Sorry. Just on the ride here. Nothing to do with you, really."

"Oh, that's fine, then." His face did not look fine.

I attempted to reassure him further, "It was fascinating. It was in an old JPL-390 in beautiful condition. A real antique."

He was turning green.

"So, you found just one?" he asked.

"Yeah, I doubt there are any other JPL-390s in the entire colony," I said. "I don't know if we will find this one's owner. Records that far back are a little sloppy."

His face's color improved a little.

He said, "I remember those days. The record-keeping was good but not centralized. It was hundreds of individual companies keeping their own records, and, as some went bankrupt, it wasn't always clear where the records went."

We finished the rest of our expected conversation, and I left.

On the way home, the driver absolutely refused to return to the JPL-390 or check any other junk piles. He had heard how the president of his company had responded to our last detour.

Even though I couldn't go look for more antiques today, I was still excited. I spent the entire trip home running through plans about renting a crawler for the coming weekend. I wanted to spend all day driving through the Forge, cataloging what I could find in the junk piles. The driver thought I was a lunatic, but not everyone can appreciate antiques.

Back in the office, I happened to pass Jane in the hallway on the way to my room. She said, "How was your audit today? Have you eaten yet?"

I said, "I already ate. The trip was great. I saw an antique. A JPL-390."

"I didn't know any of those were in the colony," she said.

"I know. It was so exciting to see one."

"I would like to see it. Maybe you could show it to me sometime."

"You don't need to wait for me. I'll send you the coordinates," I said and continued to my room.

CHAPTER 4: ANTIQUING

Most apartments were split between two floors. A basement bedroom reduced radiation exposure to zero for the third of the day you slept. An upper-story half-studio allowed for the natural light and long views that kept Earth hunger away.

The radiation exposure was limited by the two-foot-thick ceilings, the valley walls, and the lack of radiation coming through from the horizon. The little radiation that did make it through was less important since people only spent about two hours a day in the room. Overall, it was within tolerable limits.

When the weekend came, my plans to explore the Forge trash piles had to be put on hold. All accountants in the oxygen department were working overtime through the weekend due to a flurry of corrected forms we had received.

A small rebar wholesaler had liquidated a few months back and auctioned all its assets. According to the pile of forms on my desk, the purchasers incorrectly divided the oxygen. This set off a cascade of wrongly filed forms as the oxygen was resold to a dozen other companies.

It was overkill for each of those companies to then re-file their entire resource packets, but I guessed they were being careful.

The work was tedious. Most of the forms were identical to the ones they had previously filed, but every twentieth page or so had some small detail different. By the time I finished my shift on Sunday, I was bleary-eyed and ready for bed.

At least I had gotten a refund for the crawler reservation.

Walking to my room, I passed Jane at the receptionist's desk.

She said, "Jack, I went to the coordinates you sent me. I enjoyed it since I hadn't been that far from downtown before, but I didn't see the JPL-390."

I said, "I'm sorry. I thought those were the right coordinates. I'll double-check the next time I'm out there."

"You could show me," she said, playing with one of her curls.

"No. I'd feel silly driving you out there if my coordinates are wrong. I'll need to find it again first."

The residential elevator took me to the fourth floor, where my kitchen was. Soon, the smell of toast filled the room; it was about the cheapest thing to eat on Mars.

I planned for the next weekend. The Forge should be no different then, and Saturday was only six days away.

My kitchen also functioned as my living room and dining room. At 150 square feet, it was average for Mars. White walls maximized the natural light.

Instead of the Martian sunset, the building next door filled the view through the window. I told myself it made an effective radiation barrier.

I ate my toast at the table and read through my email. Spam. It was all the same stuff I had been getting on my phone for the last few days. "Congratulations, you've been selected for a free week at the Windward Resort and Hotel." I wished the FCC would find a way to stop the robocalls.

Who would ever believe those messages anyways? The Windward Resort and Hotel was the priciest hotel in the solar system. It even made the lunar hotels look cheap. It had a twenty-acre dome that contained a lawn, olive trees, vineyard, and water skis. Yes, water skis on Mars. The hotel wouldn't even return your calls if you had less than a million pounds.

The occasional billionaire visiting Mars would lease a suite for two years. The orbital frequencies of Earth and Mars hampered any manned spaceflight outside of the biennial launch windows. This made vacations to Mars that lasted less than two years impossible.

The hotel didn't sell as many rooms as its lunar competition since most people who could afford it didn't want to take two years off from their otherwise profitable lives. Occasionally, the super-rich already living on Mars would take a shorter vacation, but at £2,000 a night, it always had some vacancy.

I had driven in front of the Windward once while auditing the orchard next door. Seeing the green lawn and blue lake had made me crave Earth. I had asked permission from Darnell to audit its oxygen tanks, but he told me Mrs. Lance specifically forbade going into the Windward. If she hadn't, I would probably have audited them once a week.

I cleaned up after dinner, and my phone rang with yet another call from an unknown number. They could leave a message.

Mars used to be better about not having spam calls since the speed of light delay prevented phone calls from Earth. Apparently, Promise had grown into a real city complete with scam artists and all.

I ignored the call and walked out of the room.

The next day was Monday, and I was the first one to my desk. The pile of corrected forms was still six inches deep, but I thought I could finish them by the end of the day.

An unlabeled red envelope with a hint of perfume caught my attention. I opened it and read, "I've been hoping you would call me. I had such a relaxing time with you at the bar. Please meet me Saturday at noon at Mahoney's." It was unsigned.

I rolled my eyes and tossed the letter behind me onto Ryan's desk. People were always putting his mail on my desk by accident. I had been expecting him to be interested in going with me to the Forge on Saturday, but it seemed he would be otherwise occupied.

By evening, the remaining corrected forms were finished. Ryan had insisted on us not getting distracted. He wanted to find out who had sent the anonymous card. While there had been several women he had talked to in the bar, none of them had acted interested in that way. He worried we would end up working through the weekend again if something else came up.

The next day, I turned my light on at my desk. Normally it was off, but the light from the windows was dimmer today. Dust storms were common and had little impact on me. At the Forge, they would close down several production lines as reflectors concentrated on fewer towers.

We were an hour into the workday, and my scratch paper beside the keyboard only had a few marks on it. Ryan was humming as he typed.

I said, "What do you think of the steelworks new licensing deal?"

Ryan said, "I'm trying to work. You're not going to draw me into another discussion about random trivia."

"I think licensing the patents for their solar furnace design was a mistake. It would have been more profitable for them just to make their own Earth company," I said.

Technical solutions from Earth weren't always effective on Mars and had to be reworked here. Many of these new engineering solutions ended up being better than their Earth counterparts. One of the best examples of this was concentrated solar power.

The benefit of concentrated solar power was that once you had the reflectors, the price of power was free. The dozens of Mars companies using the technology had rapidly innovated many efficiencies, and now, even on Earth, it could compete with coal on price.

"They are already struggling to keep up with demand on Mars. They couldn't afford to split their attention," Ryan said.

"But part of the deal included engineers from their facility on Mars going to work at the new Earth project. How is that not splitting focus?"

"They were likely going to return to Earth anyways. That's what triggers most of these deals."

Having successfully engaged Ryan in the conversation, we

continued talking about the subject off and on for the rest of the work day.

Wednesday was more of the same. Jane was taking a poll about what color the exterior of the office should be when it was repainted. Its former bright green was more of a pastel green now. The rocks of the planet were so monotonous, the colonists put color on whatever structures they could.

She came to my desk and said, "I'm trying to do more around here. When I first started this job, it was a challenge, but now it's monotonous. All I do is answer phones and tell people where to email forms. I figured picking a new color for the building would be a fun change of pace."

"If you're bored, you should come out with us next time we go to Mahoney's. We have a good time," I said.

She smiled at the suggestion and said, "Maybe I will. Bars have never really been my thing, but I do want to see more of the planet. Anyways, I already spend all day with people from the office, so I should be ok doing the same at a bar."

"Great. I'll remember to tell you next time we are going out," I said.

"Thank you. So, what color do you think we should paint the building?"

I told her about a green-and-blue stripe pattern I had seen on a beetle once.

"I understand now why Darnell told me not to count your vote," she said before walking over to Susan to continue her poll.

Tomorrow would be Thursday, and there was a certification exam all the accountants in the company had to take.

The exam material was recent changes in US Treasury Department rules around money laundering and Martian commodities. I had looked through the "Interim Final Rule" for fifteen minutes when it came out last month. There were lots of technical-category adjustments but no major changes to how we needed to do our job.

Ryan had spent half a dozen evenings studying the material. Towards the end of the day, he wanted to study together some and kept asking me questions about the new rule changes. I resisted the idea of studying until I answered all his questions wrong.

I said, "Okay, maybe I underestimated this. Can you walk me through what you know tonight?"

He agreed, and we spent the evening going through all the rule changes. When we received our test results back the next day, he shook his head and said, "How come you always get more answers right? I just taught you all this last night. It's so frustrating."

I just laughed. Learning came naturally to me.

I spent Friday studying maps of the Forge. Promise was located in the valley of Eshcol, on the border of the flat Elysium Rise and the mountainous Tartarus Montes. It was in the Elysium Quadrangle with a latitude of 13.9 degrees and a longitude of 164.3 degrees.

The Forge itself was located at the west side of the valley, where it exited directly onto the Elysium Rise. I marked the coordinates I had written down for the JPL-390 and planned my search for other treasures.

Early Saturday morning, I skipped into the crawler rental office. Then I sulked out. The dealer insisted a man had called late the night before to cancel. I wasn't sure if it was an honest mistake or revenge for last weekend when I only gave them one days' notice before abandoning my reservation.

I had to go to five different garages before I could find a crawler for rent. Ironically, it was Divio's Garage that had one available. Apparently, its largest contract had recently been canceled. The owner insisted it had been without a good reason. I acted very sympathetic.

The crawler had fading plastic knobs on its console and a sticker that read, "Phobos speed limit 25 mph". It was trying to make a joke. The largest moon of Mars was named Phobos and had an escape velocity of 25.5 miles per hour. That meant if you drove twenty-six miles per hour, you would fly off the moon and leave its orbit.

The sprinter Usain Bolt could have escaped Phobos's orbit just by running.

If all you wanted was to orbit the moon, you could do it at seventeen miles per hour. Many high-school athletes achieve that during a race.

Driving out among the reflectors, I headed to the JPL-390. It wasn't there. I drove around the pile three times to make sure I wasn't in the wrong location. It must have been moved. I would have to check the oxygen records when I returned home to see who had claimed it. Hopefully, whoever it was would understand its cultural value.

I continued to check other trash piles. None had anything as interesting as a JPL-390, but there were plenty of other random tanks littered around. All were empty, as expected.

I had a suspicion that there was another JPL-390 around there somewhere. The more I thought about it, the more convinced I was. The early missions never sent only one tank of oxygen. There were always backups. A second JPL-390 should be somewhere.

After half a day of searching, I pulled out my phone and looked at the map of the area. One of the first parts of the Forge that had been built was at the northern edge of the valley, exactly where it transitioned into the Elysium Rise. The JPL-390s were likely from that time period.

I followed the road out of the valley to the west and then turned north. Each pile of discarded steel brought my hopes up. There were some interesting things in the piles but not the twin to the JPL-390.

I was beginning to give up hope when I saw a set of crawler tracks lead into a clump of boulders. On a whim, I followed them and was pleased to find a scrap pile covering half an acre. It was tucked between two boulders the size of skyscrapers. There was a modern oxygen storage tank. The gauge read empty. It must have been defective to get abandoned all the way out here.

Further searching brought me to my prize. Here it was, another JPL-390. Likely the partner to the one I found a week and a half ago.

A quick thump showed me it was empty. But it was still a treasure. I hoped it would end up in a museum one day. A close inspection of its valves showed shiny bits of metal on the threads. That was interesting. Someone had connected a hose to this tank within the last few weeks. Any longer and the shiny bits would have tarnished.

Maybe the same company that owned the other tank had checked this one hoping for free oxygen. I'd have to look at the reports later to see what they found.

There were about ten other oxygen tanks nearby, and looking at the valves on several of them showed they had also been recently accessed. Had I started an oxygen treasure hunt?

It was getting late, so I drove back to Divio's Garage and returned the crawler.

Back at the office, Ryan sat by himself, sipping a beer. Even I noticed something was wrong; he never sat by himself. Walking over to him, I asked, "How are you doing?"

"Fine," he said, not looking up.

"Find out who left the mail for you?" I said.

"No one showed up. I waited for hours."

"Sorry about that."

"It's not getting stood up that got to me. It was all the time to think about my lack of a relationship," Ryan said.

"You're great with women. I see you talking with them all the time."

"That's different from getting one to date me."

We spent the rest of the night grumbling about our lack of interested women.

CHAPTER 5: GOLD

The Mars economy was not completely self-sufficient. It produced no microchips, no pharmaceuticals, and no precision tools. All this had to be imported from Earth. In the beginning, these imports were paid for with the money investors had made on Earth. As the colony matured, investment and enthusiasm cooled. The trade balance was then maintained with exports of gold, Mars peridot, and code.

The gold fields were extremely profitable. While Earth and Mars have different geologies, the gold formations were similar. Except, no one had ever mined Mars. Under a few inches of dust, the ancient dry riverbeds still had gold nuggets just lying around. The £10 million in gold exports made this a small mine by Earth standards, but gold was so valuable per pound, the shipping cost barely factored into its profitability.

Mars peridot was a raging fad on Earth. The beautiful green stones were featured in most jewelry stores for inexplicably high prices. Merchants acquired the stones from the cult members of the Fellowship of Mars. Their exact source was unknown.

The other export of Mars was code. Programmers who wanted a life of adventure flocked to Mars. Paid by Earth companies, they provided a steady stream of cash to the colony. Working eighty hours a week for two hundred feet of living space and unlimited Martian sunsets, they were a backbone of the economy.

Sunday should have been another day spent exploring the Forge, but the bank had frozen my account due to "unusual activity." Calls to their helpline informed me I needed to call back Monday.

Since I couldn't rent a crawler, I called Ryan and asked him to meet me at Mahoney's. By the time I arrived, Ryan was talking with a woman whose graying hair put her age as early forties. A little older than Ryan, but she was holding his attention.

Ryan said, "Hi, Jack. This is Lina. I just met her while waiting for you, and I was telling her about your new hobby of exploring the junk piles out in the Forge. She says she often does similar trips."

"Nice to meet you," I said. "So, you spend a lot of time on the surface?"

Lina responded with a slight German accent, "I go about twice a week. Mostly out east in the mountains. It's so exciting."

I asked, "What kind of company does work out there?"

Ryan said, "She doesn't work for any Mars company. She's one of the un-associated programmers."

I waved over a server to order a drink.

I said, "Really? That's an expensive ticket. I don't understand people who pay their own way."

Lina said, "At one hundred thousand dollars, the ticket costs less than a house, and I get so much more out of being here. It takes twelve-hour shifts to afford it, but I get to spend my weekends exploring the surface. It's priceless."

"Telecommuting for an Earth company? I know lots of people do it, but I never understood why the companies are okay with it," I said.

"They are more than okay with it. They are enthusiastic about hiring us. Mars software engineers are known for being the best. It's mostly because you have to be well into your career to afford coming here, but the lack of distractions and the need to pay for air contribute to the work ethic," she said.

I ordered my drink, then asked, "So, if it's not for work, why do you spend time out on the surface?"

"The thrill of discovery. If you spend half a day driving in any direction, you are likely the first person to have ever set foot there," she said.

"Have you ever discovered anything?" I asked.

She laughed. "On Mars, it's not if you discover something. It's how many things you discover in a day. I was out this morning and found a rock layer that looks exactly like an Earth banded-iron formation. That should be impossible on Mars. It will likely take scientists years to figure out the chemistry behind that one. Last week, I found a lava tube with calcite crystals larger than your arm. Our understanding of the geology here is still in its infancy. It is so exciting."

The crystals sounded interesting, but I had no idea what a banded-iron formation was.

"Have you seen any JPL-390s in your travels?" I said.

"What?"

"JPL-390. They are old antique oxygen tanks. Shiny, pointy on one end, and hold about one hundred tons."

"I don't think so. Where I explore isn't anywhere near the Forge, so I don't see much scrap. You have someone hiding oxygen? I hear MARS gets picky about that."

"Not hiding. Just left over from the beginning of Promise before we started keeping track."

My drink arrived, and Ryan interjected, "I spend all my time in Promise. I want to get out and see more of the planet. Lina was saying she would be delighted to take a group of us from the office out to see some of the more interesting things she's discovered. Maybe even go explore a couple of craters she thinks may have unlisted lava tubes."

I had known Ryan for a long time and was sure he had no interest in geology. Delaying my search for the JPL-390 so Ryan could spend more time with Lina would be annoying, but a lava tube with calcite crystals the size of my arm wasn't something I was going to pass up.

"What about next Saturday?" I said. "We could get a fourth person from the office and all go for a drive."

They both agreed, and we made plans.

At work on Monday, I focused on my hobby during the breaks. The oxygen ledger showed both JPL-390s had been claimed by a gold mine up in the Cerberus Fossae.

The Cerberus Fossae was a series of parallel fissures a thousand kilometers long. From space, they looked like claw marks. They had formed from tectonic activity and were still the epicenter for frequent small Mars-quakes. At various times in the remote past, the fissures had produced vast amounts of magma and water. This provided the perfect conditions both for bringing up gold to the surface and then sorting it.

The Mars gold mines were mobile affairs. Small crawlers with metal detectors mapped out the old flow channels. Then, five-hundred-ton crawlers followed, scooping the top few feet of regolith into a drywasher like those used in the desert gold mines on Earth. The low gravity increased the amount of regolith that could be processed, and the frequent nuggets made the mine very profitable.

I didn't want to just show up at the mine unannounced. Miners on Mars were no less territorial than miners on Earth. They had literal buckets of gold stored there. It made them nervous when people went poking around.

Phone calls to the mine left me repeatedly transferred around until I was disconnected. Emails received no response at all. An audit would make a good reason to visit the mine, but Darnell would throw a fit if I used my position at MARS for personal errands.

Studying my map revealed that a few miles from the mine, there was a small vending store on the road to Promise. It was there to attract business from the miners. If I waited there, I might meet someone from the mine. Someone I could talk to about the cultural value of the JPL-390s.

On Thursday evening, I headed out to the vending store. Its sign blinked *Beer... Oxygen... Food...* It was effectively a building-sized vending machine with a room on the inside. You had to bring a pressure vessel with you, or the beer would explode when you took it outside.

Several crawlers were out front when I parked—likely miners picking up food and beer for when they went home.

The gold mine ran seven days a week, and it was just past the end of shift.

Once inside, I pretended to be reading through the beverage selection. It was all overpriced for being cheap local beer. People paid for convenience.

Everyone in the store had hardsuits with bands of reflective tape that marked them as heavy equipment operators. That's not what I wanted.

After reading labels for as long as was reasonable, I was forced to buy something not to look suspicious. I mean, *more* suspicious.

While putting the beer into my pressure cooler, a woman wearing makeup came in.

The collar of a colorful blouse seen through her faceplate marked her as a manager or secretary. Either would do. She was in the corner looking at frozen-burrito choices as I walked up to her.

"Hi, I have a question about the JPL-390," I said.

"The what?" she asked.

"The oxygen tank the mine just moved. I've been trying to contact someone about it, but no one is replying to my calls," I said, stumbling over my words before she ended the conversation.

"Does anyone ever return the Fellowship's calls?" she said and backed farther into the corner.

Following her, I said, "I'm not with the Fellowship of Mars. I had just been the one to find the tank in a junk pile and was hoping to talk to someone about its cultural value."

Talking about the cultural value of a junk pile did little to convince her I wasn't a radiation-crazed member of the Fellowship.

She slipped past me and backed into the airlock. By this point, several large men had taken notice of our conversation. They seemed to want to force me outside, but since the person fleeing my conversation was inside the airlock, that would have been counterproductive.

They didn't say anything, just stood there looking big.

"That was just a misunderstanding," I said.

No reply.

"I was just trying to get ahold of someone from the mine," I said.

"So you cornered them in a store?" said a man holding a small keg.

"Well, no one from the mine would speak to me."

The airlock was clear now, and I was backing towards it.

A man with his sun visor down repeated, "So you cornered a young woman in a store?"

"I just needed to know who to call," I said.

"So you followed a young lady into a store and cornered her?"

I didn't like the way they kept saying that.

"Look, there was no cornering."

I stepped back into the airlock and closed it. Once outside, I hurried to my crawler and left.

The reflectors of the Forge zipped past. There were no speed limits, but I was driving faster than was cautious. Swerving around a boulder, an excavator bucket was only a few feet away and swinging towards me. The axle screeched as I turned the wheel hard to the left. *Clunk.* At least the bucket didn't rip the cab off my crawler. I'd slow down once the swearing construction workers were out of sight.

It had been a long day. At home, I touched my zero-radiation plaque and fell asleep.

CHAPTER 6: EXPLORING

Software engineers on Mars made an average of $120,000 from various Earth companies. Of that, they spent $20,000 on food, air, and water. For housing, they spent $30,000 a year on two hundred feet of space. Since their income source was off-planet, they paid no taxes.

On Saturday, we were able to get a crawler rental based on Lina's employment status. Since she was paid directly by an Earth company, many businesses would accommodate her since they understood how important Earth dollars were to the economy.

It had been easy to find a fourth person for the trip. The day before, Ryan had insisted I invite Jane, but she had never mentioned liking rocks, so I didn't. Ryan had to ask her himself.

The trip began as promised. Lina drove, and Ryan sat in the passenger seat, while Jane and I rode in the back. Lina named all the varieties of rock we drove by, waving and pointing with exuberance.

I didn't understand her enthusiasm for the exact order of rock layers in the canyon walls, and it took me half the trip to realize she was saying the word epoch, and it didn't have the same meaning as epic.

Ryan must have spent the week studying since he was able to keep up with Lina's conversation. He seemed to hang on to every word she said.

Jane was in the back with me, and we often ended up in conversations of our own. She spoke of spring in Alaska and how when the snow melted, she would have to clean up an entire winter's worth of trash from her yard. Spring also brought forty-degree-Fahrenheit weather, where everyone would wear shorts and a t-shirt since they were so used to it being below freezing. That's how she knew she would be okay on Mars; she learned people could get used to anything.

For my part, I talked about the economy of Promise. How people like Lina were invaluable. They could live on a beach but instead chose to live on Mars. Their paychecks were critical for narrowing the Mars trade deficit.

Jane seemed to be interested in what I was saying, but I

knew she didn't have any real choice in a conversation partner. Ryan and Lina continued to make eyes at each other and were rapidly forgetting Jane and I were there.

When we made it to the lava tube, it made up for the blandness of the earlier geology.

I didn't like being on the surface with only my hardsuit and couldn't understand Ryan's casual attitude towards it.

The entrance to the lava tube was a steeply sloped hole in the ground where, a thousand years ago, the tube had collapsed. It was narrow enough that we had to walk single file.

Lina talked excitedly about the process that makes lava tubes. I interrupted to make everyone list back to me all sources of light on their hardsuits, so they wouldn't forget about them if we panicked in the dark.

Soon, I was behind Jane, walking down the middle of the lava tube, watching the circular gray walls of the tunnel for anything that could fall on our heads.

After walking about thirty yards, Ryan picked up a stone and threw it six feet to the wall. I yelled at him to be careful. He told me to relax.

Another thirty yards later, the tube turned a tight corner. A blue light shone ahead. Jane gasped as she rounded the bend. When I caught up, I could see why. There was a fissure cutting through the lava tube that let daylight flood in. The light passed through hundreds of deep blue crystals on its way to us, creating a mosaic of light on the walls.

Some were four feet long and a foot thick.

We turned our headlamps off and enjoyed the view for about thirty minutes before turning back to the crawler.

The second part of the day would have been drudgery without Jane being there. We drove to a small crater Lina thought, based on satellite imagery, might have another lava tube. It was just a normal crater with a boulder on the edge that cast an odd shadow.

Instead of moving on, Lina announced we were going to dig. She marked off a one-meter box with string and stakes. Then she scraped the first inch of dirt off with a shovel.

Lina said, "This is my favorite part. You never know what you are going to find."

We found a layer of dirt on top of a slightly coarser layer of dirt. When the next layer had little circular pebbles in it, Lina gasped and clapped her hands. We spent three hours like that—layer of dirt after layer of dirt, with Lina intermittently making exclamations of excitement.

Jane entertained herself by spelling out messages in the dirt with rocks in Morse code. After a few minutes, I joined her, and we played a game of taking turns adding parts to sentences.

She had already written, "Geology is a"

So I wrote, "total bore."

She removed the period and added, "except crystals."

Going to a new line, I wrote, "I want to"

She wrote, "date."

Puzzles. She was making this difficult. Where was she trying to go with this?

In all of Lina's exuberant talking, I remembered something about the importance of figuring out the date of layers of rock.

I added, "strata."

While Jane and I were playing our word games, Ryan walked over to Lina and managed half a smile.

He said, "Wow, this is a lot of fun. I'm sure it has lots of implications for… um… Mars dirt. But it's getting late, and the crawler is running low on battery. Maybe we should head back now."

She agreed, and after finishing her notes, Lina got us all back into the crawler. On the way home, she was bubbly and kept mentioning something about the dirt being unexpected. Ryan was a little strained from keeping his smile on, but overall, I was happy I'd come. The lava tube would provide an entertaining story for the rest of my life, and I'd never spent that much time talking with Jane before.

Jane was tired, and once we were back at the crawler rental, she asked me to leave with her before Ryan finished paying. I agreed. I think she was trying to give Ryan some time alone with Lina.

We lived in the same building, and I didn't want to embarrass Jane by showing up together, so at one of the stops along the way, I made an excuse about needing more flour and headed off to the shopping district.

Later that night, when I made it home, I went to my desk to check my email before going to bed. Jane was talking to Susan in her cubicle.

Jane said, "He's just so thick. He's clearly attracted. Why can't he tell when a woman's interested?"

Susan said, "Some men are just like that. The woman can take the initiative."

I didn't hear any more as I continued on to my desk. They were right, though: Ryan didn't need to pretend to like geology to spend time with Lina. She was clearly interested and would certainly hang out with him while doing a more mutually enjoyable activity.

CHAPTER 7: PRESSURE

During most days, the sky of Mars is a pink yellow, like the color of butterscotch, from the dust in the atmosphere. When the sun sets, the sky near the horizon becomes blue. On a clear day with no dust, the sky appears mostly black with a slight tint of blue, but dust-free days are rare.

The next day was Sunday. Cornering young women in stores did not seem to be the best way to find the JPL-390. I would just drive to the mine and explain the situation.

Once again, I went and rented a crawler. Being on the surface was getting more comfortable, and I only checked the latches on my helmet three times before leaving the garage.

A hundred yards out, the oxygen gauge beeped. The tank that was currently feeding the cabin was nearly out. There were three backup tanks, so I wouldn't need to return to the garage, but I wished they had filled it before I left.

Flipping the toggle should have switched tanks, but instead, it made the crawler generate a loud grating noise. Less than a second later, the crawler decompressed. All of the air in the cabin rapidly dissipated onto Mars. The minimal atmosphere in the crawler would have killed me if I had not been prepared. The hardsuit and helmet stopped my blood from boiling, but my head still started pounding from the pressure change.

After recovering from the shock of the decompression, I began safety checks. Glass panes intact? Check. Door seal intact? Check. Computer error messages? No check.

Three large, red, blinking error messages indicated there were three critical failures in the oxygen umbilical line. Opening the outer valve, I found a piece of thin chain in the first valve. It was jammed in too hard to pull out. Looking in the valve, I couldn't see how long the chain was, but it may have been long enough to jam the two secondary valves as well.

If the chain had been left under the umbilical line cap, it might have been pulled into the valves when the tanks cycled. While this could have been an accident, a piece of chain is an odd thing to accidentally leave under a cap. I wondered if Divio had realized the role I had played in his recent contract problems. Attempted murder was rare on Mars but not unheard of.

Emergency depressurization procedures call for immediately going to the nearest refuge. The computer showed a garage at ninety-one meters and an emergency shelter at eighty-four meters. I was safe in my hardsuit, and driving to the garage would let me take the normal transit system. Going to the emergency shelter would mean being stuck there until someone answered my SOS.

The choice was simple. I went to the emergency shelter. It was closer, and the emergency depressurization procedures were clear. My heart was racing, and I saw no reason to take additional risks on Mars.

The emergency shelter was just a four-foot-diameter steel can. It didn't even have an airlock, just a normal door. It swung closed when I swiped my fob and paid £1.10 for the overpriced air that then filled the room.

I didn't need the shelter's radio; the one in my suit was working just fine. The emergency services operator took my information and told me I would be picked up in two and a half hours. She was surprised I was okay; most people get lazy in crawlers and take their helmets and gloves off while driving.

The panic of having to get to safety had prevented the deeper panic on the edge of my mind from fully forming. Safe in the shelter, the chest pain and struggling to breathe started. My brain screamed I was going to die. Should improve in twenty minutes; it always had before.

The door on an emergency shelter opens inward so that when it is pressurized, the air holds the door closed. The door didn't have any locks or handles. It didn't need them. With an air pressure of fourteen pounds per square inch, the two-square-meter door was held closed with over forty thousand pounds of force. Normally, the door could only be opened by dragging the shelter into a pressurized structure.

In case of further emergency, the shelter had a valve that could vent the air pressure, letting the door open. The valve was controlled by the same computer I used to pay for the air. There were supposed to be many safety measures that prevented accidental depressurization.

I was just beginning to have enough control over my mind to start planning when the emergency shelter depressurized. It was startling. Again, there was a sucking sound, and the air left the shelter. At least it kicked me back into the focused panic of looking for safety and not a full attack.

I pushed the door open and stumbled out onto the surface of Mars. I didn't know what could have caused the emergency shelter to depressurize. There was a line of warehouses that started thirty meters away, so I headed that way.

Since the only thing that hadn't depressurized on me today was my hardsuit, I decided to walk. Walking in a hardsuit takes a lot of energy, and it chafes. But thirty meters is only thirty meters. Shorter than my recent trip through the lava tube, it only took me a minute.

No one was in the warehouse, but all structures on Mars had to be accessible in case of an emergency. Swiping my fob and getting charged £0.30 for oxygen, the airlock let me inside. I was a little frustrated at the charge. I had no intention of breathing their air. My hardsuit was not coming off.

The warehouse was a bland concrete structure with a low ceiling that stored pallets of unused Mylar. The flaking brown paint did little to improve its look.

The complaint form on my phone had almost finished downloading when an excavator rolled into view. From the force the excavator used to open the emergency shelter door with its bucket, I got the distinct feeling the driver did not have any concern for my safety. When the driver stepped out and inspected the emergency shelter, two more men followed him. Once they finished looking at the shelter, they headed to the warehouse I was in.

I decided not to find out what they wanted and left through the airlock in the back of the warehouse. It made a swoosh as it cycled open and closed. Running another hundred meters, I made it into a second warehouse and was charged another £0.30 as I used my fob to enter the building. Piles of rebar this time. At least the paint was brighter.

Within a minute, three men in hardsuits came around the first warehouse and headed straight in my direction. I could see them through the airlock window, but how did they know where I was?

Another airlock cycle and then another hundred meters. When the three men in hardsuits came around the warehouse instead of through it, I made a guess at how they were tracking me. My phone, the computer in my hardsuit, and the auxiliary computer were all piled on the floor. Everything that had a radio. Maybe that was how they were tracking me.

All buildings on Mars had multiple airlocks. I found another back way out and continued on another fifty meters, skipping a warehouse and ducking into a structure used for the maintenance of a well. My fob was charged £0.20 this time. At least it was a better deal.

My pursuers didn't even look at the warehouse I'd skipped. They ran straight towards the well house.

I understood. It was the fob, not the radio. Chafing, I ran out the back and to another warehouse. This time, I fobbed the airlock but didn't go in as the doors cycled. Hiding around a boulder and detaching my sun visor to use as a mirror, I watched as my pursuers entered the warehouse I had just fobbed.

Circling around a row of yet more warehouses, I ran back to the crawler. It wasn't pressurized anymore, but it could move a lot faster than I could.

The transit lines and every building in the colony would require me to use my fob to get in the door. I couldn't get home safely without help. The radio in the crawler connected me with a disinterested emergency operator: *I was being chased by a group of large men? Had they hurt me? Even talked to me? Had they at least shaken a big stick at me?*

I stressed that my emergency shelter had depressurized. She asked if the men had been there when it happened? Why was I in an emergency shelter if I had a hardsuit and was only ninety meters from a garage that was connected to the transit network?

She was not sure a crime had been committed. She told me to wait for an FBI agent at the nearest garage, they would be there shortly.

The first three garages I passed had miners loitering in front of them, so I waited in the crawler well outside of Divio's Garage. When the FBI agent came, Divio was enraged; he blamed me for the chain in the oxygen valves. The FBI agent took notes and seemed to think this was all an accident. He asked me several times if I had ever seen the chain before or had any reason to try to jimmy open the valves.

He might have trusted my story more if I hadn't explained in so much detail how panicked I was by the decompression.

Two miners driving a small excavator were found. They said they had heard the SOS about someone who was stranded by a depressurization. After checking several buildings for survivors, they had given up. No, they hadn't seen anyone else. They said it had just been the two of them, and the fob records confirmed it. They reported they had damaged the emergency shelter in their haste to try to open the door and were relieved to find it unoccupied.

My hardsuit went into my bedroom with me, but at least I wasn't wearing it when I touched the no-radiation plaque on the wall and fell into bed.

CHAPTER 8: ON THE RUN

Father Gray had a secret. He was going to build his cathedral. When the Catholic Church had registered for thirty acres in the middle of Promise, they had provided enough funds to build a moderately sized church on Earth. That would have built a small chapel on Mars.

Instead of building the chapel, he rented a warehouse for services and had faith he could build his cathedral in time. He used all the remaining funds to purchase a contract for steel from Marucible LLC for £120 per ton to be delivered in one year.

This was the early days of Promise when every industry was just beginning, and optimism ran high. Marucible LLC ran into all the typical delays of a large project. When it came time to deliver the steel, it was still costing them £230 per ton to produce. They gladly bought the contract back for a £50 per ton penalty.

Father Gray didn't want to buy further steel since the prices were high, so he instead spent his now-increased funds on sheets of clear glass. This contract was honored and delivered. A month later, the great greenhouse boom started, and glass prices tripled. He didn't have a steel frame to put his glass on, so he sold it.

When the greenhouses started to produce large quantities of rubber, the amount of concrete needed for construction decreased. When the price dropped, Father Gray bought enough concrete for his cathedral.

Now, he waits and has faith. One day, he will build his cathedral, and Mars will know the devotion of man to God.

Sleeping underground meant morning arrived on a timer. The lights gradually turned to full power over fifteen minutes. I felt whichever engineer had built that timer without user controls should be exiled from Mars.

I covered my head with a quilt I had brought from Earth. It was the reason I had learned to sew. My mother had made it for me when I was a child, and the corners kept coming undone.

When my alarm went off, I stumbled over to the bathroom. A made-on-Mars toothbrush, toothpaste, and floss waited for me. The floor was dark blue, the walls neon yellow, and the ceiling bright pink.

A few months ago, when Ryan had seen my color choices, he had called me mental. He still brought it up regularly in conversation. I kept telling him damp underground spaces need some livening up.

When Jane had heard about it, she had asked to come down to my bedroom to see it, but I didn't need anyone else mocking me.

Once my teeth were brushed and I was showered, I put on slacks and a button-up shirt. No tie. Mars was casual.

At my desk, I spent most of the day distracted by thoughts of the night before. The FBI hadn't seemed concerned about anything that had happened. They were the experts. I had even called Bruce to get his take on everything. He only told me, "I can't comment on an ongoing investigation. But if this has been reported to the FBI agents on Mars, then you don't need to worry about it. We always sort everything out."

I was eventually able to distract myself by pulling Ryan into a conversation about patent lawyers. He had been working hard, but when I insisted patent lawyers would get more Mars business living on Earth than Mars, he was unable to resist telling me how stupid that idea was. With the conversation started, neither of us finished much work.

When we clocked out, I expected Ryan to want to continue this discussion over toast.

Instead, he said, "Not today. I'm trying to get healthier. Going to the gym."

He had played football in high school, and while not fat now, he was out of shape.

That night was spent worrying as I reflected on the prior day.

The next day, Susan walked into my cubicle and said, "Craig solved an anomaly at a toilet paper factory. We are all going out tonight."

Ryan said, "I can't go, but what caused the anomaly?"

She said, "A change in the cement recipe had absorbed more CO_2 than normal. This led to calculation errors. The O_2 level was actually unchanged. What about you Jack, are you coming?"

I said, "I'm staying home today also. That decompression I had is making me nervous about leaving the building."

"Too bad, without you, we'll have to leave earlier to get seats," she said.

Ryan was still laughing two minutes after she went back to her cubicle. When he stopped laughing, I said, "Nice of you to stay back with me."

Ryan said, "I'm actually going to the gym again today."

I raised an eyebrow and said, "Really? You never miss a chance to go out with the group."

"I'm trying to get back in shape," he said.

I just kept my eyebrow raised and waited.

He said, "Okay. Lina also uses the gym in the evenings."

Resisting childish teasing as he got ready to go, I settled down with a book for the evening. Today's book was *The*

Martian by Andy Weir. Such a classic. I hoped it would keep my mind off my recent troubles.

For the next week, I did not leave the building. The FBI may have thought there was no foul play during my last excursion, but I felt otherwise.

On Monday, Darnell walked into my cubicle wearing his typical button-up shirt with a pocket protector. Pocket protectors may not be stylish, but frayed pockets were worse.

"Your turn to do a random audit," he said.

"You sure? I just had one at the concrete company," I said, sitting at my desk.

"Everyone else has had their turn since then."

"I'd really like not to leave the building right now."

"Is this about those decompressions? You need to get over that. The FBI has looked into it, and there was nothing suspicious besides some faulty maintenance," he said.

"It just makes me nervous to ride in a crawler so soon."

"You won't start feeling normal until you start acting normal. You have your assignment. I expect you to do it."

With that, he left.

I turned around to Ryan, who was at his desk. I asked, "Can you fob me onto the transit line?"

"What for?" he asked. He was browsing oxygen records from a steel factory.

"I told you the story about what happened last time. I don't trust some of those billionaires on Sunside Row. All those stories about people going there and never coming back. I just want to start my trip without showing up on the computer," I said.

"Are you a conspiracy theorist now? No one I know has ever disappeared. In fact, no one I know knows anyone who has disappeared. What would they have against you? You're a cog in their machine," he said.

"I know, but can you do it anyways?"

"Sure. If I'm lucky, I'll run into Lina and make evening plans over a quick lunch."

"Thanks. And it's not luck if you text someone first."

I was nervous about leaving the building, but the FBI, Ryan, and Darnell had all reassured me my fears were all in my head. Bruce had insisted it was from the jar my brain got when my crawler decompressed.

I was mostly convinced. I wanted to be completely convinced. I had a plan to reassure myself.

Ryan used his fob on the transit line, and I rode it to a garage that didn't belong to Divio. There were no problems finding a rental since it was a weekday. I triple-checked the crawler before pulling off the lot. Then I drove fast along the most-used paths. If anyone was trying to follow me, they would have a difficult time.

The audit I was doing was at a rubber orchard in an industrial area with numerous small factories and warehouses. Instead of going directly to the orchard, I went to a more remote portion of the industrial park.

Three warehouses on the left whizzed by, but they had nowhere to hide my crawler. A little further and there was a single warehouse about two hundred yards from a boulder pile. Perfect. My fob cycled the airlock, but I didn't go in. Quickly, I drove to the boulder pile and parked my crawler out of sight.

My phone, despite being a few years old, recorded the airlock clearly. The 30x camera zoom had been standard for a while.

Nothing happened for twenty minutes as the condensation dripped down the inside of the warehouse's windows.

Due east, a small blue light appeared in the sky and began to grow brighter. It was the methane blue of a rocket engine. As it got closer, it transitioned to the yellow glow of fuel-rich combustion. At about two hundred meters overhead, the plume turned green, the color of engine-rich combustion.

Fuel-rich means burning excess fuel in the combustion chamber. Engine-rich means burning excess engine components in the combustion chamber. It's an old joke from the beginning of interplanetary travel. Copper burns green, and many internal components of rocket engines are made of copper.

It was close enough for me to tell it was a standard cargo hauler—a fifty-meter cylinder with one pointed end and the shine of stainless steel.

The rocket was twisting now since the engines could no longer stabilize it.

Helpless. I stood behind a two-meter rock as a fifty-meter ship that was 90 percent explosive fuel by weight hurtled in my direction.

The malfunctioning rocket slammed into the ground at over fifty meters per second and exploded. It hit on the other side of the warehouse, but the shock wave was still jarring.

When I stopped cowering, the condensation in the windows of the warehouse had disappeared, a sure sign of decompression.

I had been expecting a group of miners to show up or another explosive decompression. I hadn't been expecting someone to drop a spaceship on my head. This left me in a bit of a pickle. While it should be easy to prove this was a murder attempt given everything that had happened recently, it could be impossible to prove who had programmed the ship.

A ship old enough to malfunction may have had a dozen different owners in the last forty years. There would be hundreds of employees at those corporations who could have done this.

If I went home, what was stopping them from dropping another ship on my head? Anywhere I fobbed in, they could find me. I could radio into the emergency operator, but that hadn't done me any good last time.

The ship's malfunction was going to cause me more trouble than its programmer. If it had destroyed the warehouse, I could just leave and hide. It would have taken them days to figure out I was still alive. As things stood, it would only take them minutes.

They had the resources to drop a ship on my head, so they had the resources to buy satellite imaging every time one passed overhead.

I had a crawler but no way to hide it. In the dust on a calm day like this, they could track me even without the satellites.

I needed to make it to the shopping district. It had miles of tunnels I could hide in. My hardsuit was indistinguishable from other hardsuits. As long as I didn't fob in anywhere, I could lose my pursuers in the crowd.

Clunk, went the pedal as I pressed it to the floor. If someone was going to catch me, they were going to have to move fast. Luckily, the edge of the shopping district was only five miles away.

No more ships fell out of the sky, and no one was at the elevator as it came into view. At the elevator, I fobbed in for

£2.50, and it filled with air. They would know I was here, but once the elevator got to the bottom floor, I would have miles of branching tunnels to hide in.

The shopping district of Promise was completely below ground. It had taken a lot of convincing for the planning council to approve it, as it was similar to the failed colony of Plymouth. What convinced them was the promise of greenery.

Hanging vines covered the walls. Flowers lined every walkway. Jasmine curled up the pillars and filled the whole district with its floral scent. Water gurgled from hundreds of fountains. It was underground, but it felt like a park.

The crowd was thick, and I headed to a busy intersection up ahead. The hardsuit chafed, but it gave me an excuse to keep my helmet on. Two random turns later, I felt confident I was safe. I would have walked farther without the chafing, but this would do.

The concrete bench had been overrun with a red climbing rose. The hardsuit stopped the thorns. I sat and thought, watching people walk in and out of the hardware store in front of me.

Whoever had dropped that ship on me must have been desperate. It was such an open and grand way to commit murder.

What had I done to make them desperate? Did I know

something they didn't want me to know? Had an audit at work gotten too close to something hidden?

I didn't feel safe going to the FBI since they had ignored my previous complaints. Bruce would just swagger around and give me his I-can't-comment-on-an-ongoing-investigation line. Anyways, they didn't have anything that could stop a ship from flattening me. I needed to find out what was going on.

An advantage of disappearing would be that the FBI would take all this seriously. Anyone looking for me would only find a single fob record after a ship fell out of the sky and destroyed the building I was supposedly in.

Darnell would be worried and make a stink if the FBI didn't look for me. Mrs. Lance might even get involved. I had disappeared while on an official audit. She would take that personally.

People often spent their evenings relaxing in the tunnels due to all the flowers. I blended in, and a few hours would hopefully let my pursuers give up on finding me. My sun visor hid my face, making me look like I was napping. That was common here, and I didn't intend to actually fall asleep, but the adrenaline was wearing off.

I was not dead when I woke up, so that was good. No one had found me here. I needed a plan.

The lady I had cornered in the vending store had assumed I

was with the Fellowship of Mars when I asked about the JPL-390. Maybe they were involved in this somehow.

On Earth, a full 1 percent of people suffer from schizophrenia or other psychotic diseases. On Mars, about 0.5 percent did. That was high. The majority of people who moved to Mars were in their thirties or forties. Schizophrenia frequently develops earlier than that. It's hard to travel to Mars if you're psychotic.

Radiation in the form of galactic cosmic rays had a nasty way of randomly killing cells in your brain. This was different from solar energetic particles, which were more numerous and caused classic radiation damage that diffusely affected tissues.

The risks from galactic cosmic rays were minimized by various forms of radiation shielding, but unlike solar energetic particles, some always made it through. If the brain cells they killed were particularly important, you could end up psychotic or confused.

The Fellowship of Mars was made up of these people. It was unclear what led so many psychotic people to join the group, but it was probably the Earth hunger. Everyone on Mars felt it to some extent, but psychosis complicated things.

The Fellowship of Mars had a central premise: to be at home on Mars and stop longing for Earth, you must walk naked across the surface. Not in a building but beneath the open sky. Like I said, they were crazy.

Crazy, but with lots of money. Enough billionaires had cracked that the group was well funded.

Their main camp was forty miles due south of Promise on a rectangular mesa. On Earth, that would have been a simple three-day hike for me. On Mars in a hardsuit, it would be impossible. I needed a crawler, and I needed one without using my fob.

Security on Mars was lax. Everything was tracked so heavily in the computers it was hard to get away with a crime.

The reason automated service vehicles had cabins was so they could be used as emergency pressure shelters. If I got to one, I could use the safety override to take control of it. It would immediately alert its owner when I initiated the override, but that was easy to get around. I would just have to remove the radio first. If taken in the morning as it began its automated loop, no one would notice it was missing for about three hours.

My nap had brought me too late in the evening, and the shopping district was going to shut down soon. My hardsuit had only five hours of air, and I had to make it through the night. Luckily, I was an oxygen accountant.

It was time to go. The elevator opened, and I joined the

crowd as everyone piled on. No fobbing needed since there was no price to leave. Everyone was in a hardsuit since this elevator went directly to the surface. I blended in perfectly.

It was a long chafing walk to old downtown. This was the area the planners had wanted to be the vibrant center of the city. All the leading companies that started the colony had land here. Most of those companies were now bankrupt, and this area had been partially abandoned. The occasional corporate office dotted the area, but it was mostly empty lots or half-finished structures. It had been the second wave of companies on Promise that had become profitable.

Being one of the oldest parts of the city, many of the oxygen tanks here were not networked. You used your fob to buy air, and then once a week, someone came through and downloaded the history and charged your account. This would be perfect for me today. I could buy air with my fob, but nobody would know for a week.

I found one of the tanks I was looking for. Wanting a full night's rest, I plugged in my umbilical hose and just slept right there on the ground. The air to breathe would be pricey, but the electricity to keep me warm would be somewhat more reasonable. At this point, I was just happy to try to sleep.

Trying was all I was able to do for several hours. Lying on the ground with only my hardsuit between me and Mars, I couldn't turn my brain off. All my recent activity had made me trust my hardsuit more, but Mars was just too close.

Eventually, I fell asleep.

The refill station I had picked was tucked into an alley, and I hadn't thought anyone would notice me since this part of the town was so empty.

Slowly awakening. What was happening?

Tap. Tap. "Hello there," my short-range radio transmitted.

"Huh?" I said.

"Do you need any help?" said the soft voice.

A black hardsuit was standing over me. Its only marking was a two-inch white square on the neck.

"No, I'm fine," I said.

"You spent the whole night out here in full radiation exposure." It wasn't a question.

I didn't have a good response.

He said, "Come with me. I'm only going a little way down the road, and I won't charge you for the air. There should also be some toast."

Did I look that bad? I hadn't eaten since yesterday, and toast did sound appealing.

He helped me unclip the umbilical hose and then pulled my hand so I could stand. Then we walked down the dirt road. Or, he walked while I hobbled.

"You're Father Gray, aren't you?" I said.

"Yes. I wasn't sure you were awake when I first introduced myself. What gave it away now?" he said with a grin.

"The photos on the news," I said.

Father Gray was famous for being the only poor person on the planning council. To be on the planning council, a person had to be able to invest £2 million on Mars or be a representative of a company that could. The Catholic Church was a big enough entity, and Father Gray was the highest-ranking Catholic on Mars.

None of the bishops were willing to come to Mars. Father Gray would likely have been a bishop himself by now, but he would have had to travel to Earth for that. He wouldn't spend the two years it would take to get there and back. Earth was too far away to use the same launch window for a round trip.

"Your leg okay?" he asked.

"Just chafing, I can never get these suits to fit right," I said.

"Don't use them much, then?"

"Only about once or twice a month."

"An adventurer? Come to Mars to work eighty hours a week so twice a month you can go exploring this new planet?" he said.

"No, I came for the money. I plan to retire back to Earth in about ten years and live comfortably. I don't think I could deal with the Earth hunger longer than that. Where else could I work for fifteen years and then be able to retire to a Florida beach in comfort? Don't get me wrong, coming to Mars has been great. I wouldn't give that up for anything, but I want to swim in the ocean and walk through a field again."

I was opening up more than I usually did, but he listened well.

"That plan seems to have hit a speed bump if you can't afford oxygen. Don't look surprised at me like that. You're not the first person to come out here for oxygen because the tanks aren't networked. Though most people just fill a container and don't sleep exposed out in the open," he said.

I guess that's what it looked like. Mars offered all the same vices as Earth, and, occasionally, a gambling debt or heroin bill became so high not even a Martian salary could pay it. Going broke on Mars meant getting shipped back to Earth. Then the debt really became insurmountable.

He continued, "People will go to great lengths to not get shipped off Mars. Which is funny given how fast everyone else flees this place."

"People like it here," I said.

"You don't like it enough to stay," he said.

"True. But lots of people talk about wanting to live here and be buried here," I said.

"Any of your friends?" he asked.

I stopped and thought. Ryan was going back to Earth. He always talked about Texas. Jane always asked me about how I liked Florida; she was from Alaska and said she was thinking about somewhere warmer. Darnell might have been staying on Mars, but he never talked about it one way or the other.

The only people who I knew for sure were staying long-term were Jamie and Benny from water accounting. They were always looking at prefab retirement homes they could place in the mountains.

"Two people I can think of out of about twenty. But that can't be typical," I said.

He said, "It is. About ninety percent of people who come here plan to return to Earth. Even with everything we do to make this place hospitable, most people don't want to stay. People come for the money or the adventure. When they grow old, they have the money and are less interested in the adventure. Then they go home."

We walked in silence for a minute before he spoke again, "The planning committee downplays this aggressively. At the last meeting, there was even talk about opening a free old folks' home to convince people to stay. They charge you for the air you breathe but want to pay for your retirement. That's how you know they are desperate."

I thought about this and then said, "But the population has been growing steadily."

"That's the aggressive recruiting on Earth. About thirty percent of the planning committee's budget goes to advertising. If you thought there were a lot of ads before you left, you should see them now. It's worse than an election cycle," he said.

"So, people stay fifteen to twenty years and then head back to Earth to be replaced by more recruits?" I said.

"The average is ten years. If you look at the population graphs from forty years ago, Promise grew at an exponential rate. After twenty years, that slowed, and over the last three years, it has become a trickle. This year's census numbers haven't been released yet, but they show Promise has only grown by four hundred and fifty-seven people," he said.

"That's less than 0.15 percent. But most buildings here are crowded. I wouldn't mind if the population actually decreased a little," I said.

"That would be a disaster. Promise's economy would be very sensitive to a recession. Since we normally lose a fifth of our population every two years, we can't afford to have companies stall their hiring."

"If the economy slows and companies stop bringing in employees from Earth, then our population would drop rapidly?" I said.

"Yes, and even more importantly, outside investment would stop. So much business is dependent on there being people to sell shelter, air, water, food, and electricity to. A decreasing population would remove the possibility of profits from too many businesses," he said.

He continued, "The planning committee will spin our barely growing population as the colony having matured. That we have reached our steady-state population and will continue here for some time. That would be true if we were replacing people with children and not fresh workers from Earth. There are almost no families here. If you watch the news, you have likely seen literally every child on the planet," he said.

"To convince a woman to have a child here is a hard sell," I agreed. I would never do it. Fifteen years of radiation was tolerable, but seventy years would be too much. The child would either have to live underground or accept early dementia.

We talked for a while more. Eventually, I asked him why he thought Mars was important.

He said, "Haven't you read Genesis? 'God blessed them and said to them, 'Be fruitful and increase in number; fill the earth and subdue it.'"

He continued, "See, it was a blessing that we were told to fill the Earth. I don't think this applies to one planet alone. We will be blessed in our expansion onto many worlds. It is a blessing to be able to do this, and we shall be blessed in doing it."

He continued, "Now tell me, what trouble brings you to sleep under the stars breathing borrowed oxygen?"

"I'm not in any trouble—at least not in that way. I haven't done anything wrong. It's just that some men are after me."

Silence.

"I didn't do anything to them. I don't even know why they are after me," I said.

The silence then continued for an uncomfortable period.

Soon, he stopped and turned us onto a driveway. We were at a warehouse with an airlock big enough for a crawler.

"Here we are," he said. "Let's get you inside so I can see this man who is pursued for no reason."

The sign over the airlock read, "Saint Mary Catholic Church."

Inside was an area designed to hold thirty crawlers, though there was only one there. We continued through one more door and then were in a large room filled with carved wood, statues, and crucifixes. He led me to a small side door, and we entered a room with a bed, dresser, toaster, teapot, and two small chairs.

We doffed our hardsuits in the small room. My leg was

91

worse than I thought; I had worn away enough skin to have a three-inch spot of blood on my pants.

I bandaged my leg with the supplies he provided while he put on tea and began the toast.

"So, what do you plan on doing next?" he asked.

"I don't really want to talk about it," I said.

"Sometimes talking about things helps put them in perspective," he said.

"I'm not Catholic. I don't have any obligation to confess to you," I said.

"Confession is only for sins. You've already established you didn't do anything wrong," he said.

"You don't see me prying into your business. What if I kept asking about what happened between you and Bishop Thomas? You wouldn't like that, would you?"

Father Gray oversaw several dozen churches in the independent Catholic mission of Mars and was directly under the jurisdiction of Rome. Any priest traveling to Mars to set up a church should have coordinated with Father Gray.

About three years ago, Bishop Thomas was on Earth when he sent a priest to Mars to travel with a wealthy Brazilian. He didn't even tell Father Gray he was coming. When this was discovered, he refused to work with the mission.

It had been a bit of a scandal. The news was talking about

the conflict in the local Catholic church the entire time the incoming priest was traveling to Mars. There had been talk of official sanctions.

Once the priest actually arrived, it dropped out of the news. I didn't know what had happened and assumed he didn't want to talk about it.

Father Gray laughed. Then he said, "Catholics have always run the social services, and knowing what is going on helps with that. I'll take your implied deal. When Bishop Thomas's priest arrived, I bought him fresh Mars licorice and introduced him to the other priests in the area."

"They agreed for him to join your mission and no longer be under Bishop Thomas? I didn't see anything about that in the news. The stories just kind of stopped."

"No, not at all. He still is under Bishop Thomas."

"But that violates the integrity of your mission. It is a blatant affront," I said.

"The real reason why there are titles, territories, and orders of precedence in the church is to give us something to forgive others for. It also gives me a chance to practice humility. Why drag him before Rome? I have no need to defend the dignity of the church. God does that."

He continued, "I kept my end of the bargain. Now, what is your story?"

Not being particularly pleased with the conversational corner I had wedged myself into, I told him my story. I finished by admitting to my plan of stealing an automated service vehicle and visiting the Fellowship of Mars.

"Stealing? I thought you hadn't done anything wrong," he said.

"I haven't done it yet, and I feel it's justified," I said.

"Everyone always does. How about I rent you my crawler but don't put the charge through for one week?"

"That would simplify my life. Thank you so much."

"Don't thank me yet. When you look at the rate I'm charging you, consider it a tithe," he said.

CHAPTER 9: FELLOWSHIP OF MARS

The Mars atmosphere was so thin you couldn't tell it apart from a complete void if you stepped out into it. You would lose consciousness within fifteen seconds while feeling the liquid on your tongue boil. Fluid would rush out of all orifices and also boil. Soon, your skin would stretch tight as your intestines inflated and air bubbles formed in your tissue.

Surprisingly, early NASA experiments show that as long as you were repressurized in less than three minutes, you would likely survive with no deficits.

As we left the nave and entered the parking area, I pointed around at the building and asked, "How do you pay for all this?"

"The same way Catholics on Earth do. About sixteen percent of people on both Mars and Earth are Catholic. Of that, about forty percent come to church. And of that group, about sixty percent give money."

I checked all the valves on the crawler, then stepped in and finished talking with the priest before I closed the door.

"Thanks for playing out the Good Samaritan story," I said.

"You forget I'm a priest. If I was acting out that story, I would have had to leave you in the ditch," he said, laughing.

I closed the door and drove out of the airlock. Following the road east out of the valley of Eshcol, I saw more greenhouses and light manufacturing. Turning south, the lines between boulders, mesas, and mountains began to blur as outcroppings of all sizes and geometry became more common.

The GPS for this area had maps with a pixel resolution larger than the crawler. While I couldn't get lost, driving involved a lot of decisions about which slopes looked less likely to flip me over. Eventually, I found a well-worn track that led in the general direction I wanted to go.

Following it, a rectangular mesa came into view. It was a mile and a half wide and five miles long. I knew from its reputation that this was the Fellowship's camp. The only place the wall's slope was shallow enough to drive up was on its north face.

Once on the mesa, I was surprised to find no gate, no parking lot, and no buildings. Industrial equipment was everywhere, and much of it was upside down or on its side. Of the hundred crawlers I could see, I doubted if more than ten ran. Sorted shirts, bottles, computers, plates, and other household goods were in piles on the ground in an order whose purpose I could not comprehend.

None of the people walking or lounging in hardsuits paid me any attention. Some even wore softsuits. Insane; they were not designed for continuous use in a near void.

The track continued farther along the mesa, and I kept going, looking for something to signify central authority or a visitors center. There was neither, but in the distance, a collection of hundred-ton oxygen tanks came into view. I drove that way.

Limping between the dozens of building-sized tanks, I checked gauges and kept a running tally in my head. There were more than twelve thousand tons of oxygen here. And I could see other oxygen tanks in the distance.

There couldn't be more than a thousand members of the Fellowship of Mars. This was over ten years of oxygen. Where did it come from? I would surely have noticed reports of this much oxygen being transferred to the Fellowship.

The ground here was flat and well-tracked. Some of the oxygen tanks had tarps taped to them, making little tents. I walked into the first tent, and there was a man sitting on a crate with a chisel and hammer in his hands. All around him were white rock chips matching the color of the stone in front of him.

"Hello," I said.

"You found me. I'm not giving it back. It's my squirrel," he said while waving his chisel in my direction.

"Do you know how long these oxygen tanks have been here?" I said, gesturing to the wall of his tent.

"You're being squirrely. Maybe there's a squirrel inside you, too. I'm trying to get one out of this rock. But you might be easier," he said, standing up.

"Never mind. I think I'll keep looking on my own," I said as I backed out of the tent.

Skipping three pink tents to put some distance between me and the man with the chisel, I proceeded to a bright green tent. Inside was a small cot, a lamp wearing sunglasses, and a knit hat.

I was about to leave when the back wall of the tent opened, and a man walked in. He said, "Hello, is this your tent?"

"No, I thought this was your tent," I said.

"That's odd. You were inside, and I walked in. Why would it be my tent?" he said, going to sit on the cot.

"Do you know how long these oxygen tanks have been here?" I asked.

"Oxygen tanks? Where?" he said, leaning against the sidewall of the tent, which was a three-story-tall oxygen tank.

"That tank you're leaning on right now. How long has it been there?"

"Oh, I think it's been there a while. That's why they put the planet here, to keep it at the right angle."

"Is there anyone else around here I could talk to?" I asked.

"No, I'm by far the sharpest person here. All the others went to the initiation."

I had been stepping backwards, preparing to leave the tent. Instead, I asked, "Where's that?"

"By the cricket rock. Just head out the door and follow Murphy's Lance for a while until you get to the little rock, then turn right."

"You wouldn't mind showing me, would you?" I said, quite sure I would be unable to follow those directions.

"No, I don't go to the initiations anymore. They never let the bodies lay long enough. But Jiminy is going in just a minute. I'll take you to him."

There had to be someone around here who could answer a question straight. Otherwise, how did they buy things or manage not to kill themselves?

The man I was being led to was in a softsuit and wearing a sandwich board that read, "The End is Near. Don't forget to give him at least 2 pennies."

My guide introduced me to Jiminy, who then led me east.

I was avoiding conversation until he volunteered, "Don't be too disturbed by the people in the camp. When strangers come through, they often act crazy so they don't have to talk to them. They are good people, and God will take care of them when the end comes."

He said this as he smeared lipstick across his face shield, giving himself red eyebrows.

"Do you know how long those oxygen tanks have been there?" I asked, stepping gingerly over a dog-sized rock. The padding the priest had given me for my hardsuit helped a lot, but the skin I had chaffed still stung.

"We've been getting a lot more over the last couple of weeks. Comes in with the other scrap we buy. I don't know why the city folk started storing their oxygen tanks in scrap piles, but they are a little crazy up there."

"Do you know who you buy them from?" I asked.

"Dogger would know that. He takes care of most of the financials for this area of the camp. I don't know why he buys so much oxygen. He says he gets a good price, but with the end coming so soon, what's the point of storing all this here?"

As we kept walking, another man joined us. He wore a tattered hardsuit.

Jiminy said, "Hi Patrick. Where are you going today?"

"Obviously wherever the most important thing is," Patrick said.

"What?" I said.

"So I can do it. One should always do the most important thing. That's its definition," he said.

The path we were following forked in three directions. Jiminy stopped and adjusted his sign. He couldn't get it to his liking, so he took it off and began fiddling with the shoulder strap.

Patrick stopped with us, and Jiminy asked him, "Have you ever been to China?"

"No, why?" he said.

"I'm trying to figure out if it really exists. I've never been there, but I've seen it on maps," Jiminy said.

"It's a real place. Like you said, it's on the maps," I said.

"Just because two or three men decided to draw a squiggly circle and write the word China in the middle seems like a silly reason to believe in something as unlikely as a country with over a billion people and limited civil unrest."

I said, "They have one of the most advanced space programs in the world and deliver about a third of the freight to Promise. They are real."

"Have you spoken to anyone who came from China on one of their rockets?" Jiminy said.

"Yes, several."

"What proof did they offer that they had come from China?"

"I didn't ask them for any," I said.

Patrick said, "This is silly. You walk around with a sandwich board saying the end is coming. What proof do you have of that?"

"I have much better proof than your evidence for China. Eleven men swore to seeing the divinity of Jesus. Ten proved their statements with willing deaths and the eleventh with a willing exile. All their testimony is written down. We've made over five billion copies of their witness statements if you would like one," Jiminy said.

"I'm not sure if that passes the sniff test," Patrick said.

Twenty minutes later, we were still at the crossroads as Jiminy listed out everything he didn't think passed the sniff test. The list included bags of water that could talk, the universe, the color blue, a modern country that has twenty-five million people but only 605 who use the internet, any reality in which it is possible to prove Godel's proof, cotton candy being invented by dentists, evolution, and my armpits.

He said, "Those are all real but seem unlikely. Your problem isn't that you find God as an unlikely explanation for the universe; it's that you find the universe itself unlikely, so any explanation for it will not pass your sniff test."

Having an opening in the conversation, I said, "You mentioned a man named Dogger earlier. Where is he?"

"Next to the rock that's next to Dogger," Jiminy said.

I debated just picking a path and walking down it, but I didn't like the idea of being alone out here. I waited until he got his sandwich board back together and stopped quarreling with Patrick. Eventually, Patrick took a path to the left, and I followed Jiminy to the right.

Feeling much less frustrated when he wasn't talking, I walked in silence.

We eventually made it to the edge of the mesa. There, we found the only pressurized building I had seen in the camp. It was mostly glass, about eight feet by eight feet. There were two airlocks: a typical one on the east wall and a peculiar one on the west wall.

Most airlocks were designed so several people could fit in them. This one looked like it could hold one skinny person.

About thirty people in hard- or softsuits circled the structure. They seemed to be waiting on the man who was taking off his hardsuit between the two airlocks.

Jiminy took a place in the circle, and I tried to start a conversation with a woman standing beside him. She quieted me and pointed at the man, so I stood and watched with everyone else.

The man in the building was now only in his underwear and was squeezing into the small airlock in the east wall. When the first door of the airlock closed behind him, everyone cheered.

He stood there for a few minutes with sweat running off his brow. Eventually, he started trying to open the door behind him that he had just come through. It would not budge. He couldn't move much; the glass door in front of him leading out onto the surface was only about sixteen inches from the door he had just come through.

"He can't make himself do it," came the chatter over the short-range comms.

"He's got no choice now."

"Look at him sweating."

"There, he's turning the valve. I bet he overdoes it and can't even get out the door."

A small gauge on his airlock showed the pressure was two pounds per square inch. That's less pressure than on the top of Mount Everest. It must have been pure oxygen for him to be conscious.

Next, his hand gripped a lever, and he stood motionless for a full five minutes.

When the lever was pulled, the pressure gauge dropped to zero in one second, and the glass door flew open. The man inside got two steps forward before he hit the ground. Everyone watched for a full minute as his abdomen inflated to double its normal size, and his bodily fluids boiled around him.

He wasn't moving when two men in hardsuits dragged him back into the airlock on the west side of the building.

I pulled down my sun visor so no one could see the vomit inside my suit.

The crowd began to mill around and talk, so I approached one of the more normal-looking hardsuits and tapped it on the shoulder. When it turned around, she was a woman in her sixties. She had wrinkly skin and unkempt hair.

"Do you know who Dogger is?" I asked.

"Another one for the ritual? It will take us an hour to get the last initiate fully resuscitated and the airlock ready again."

Throwing up my hands, I said, "No. I'm just here to talk to Dogger about oxygen tanks and money."

"That's a pity. You'll never feel at home here until you walk naked across the surface. Dogger is over there," she said, gesturing to her right.

I walked over to Dogger. He was fiddling with a valve on the back of another man's hardsuit. Seeing me, he took off his right glove and held out his hand while saying, "I'm Dogger. Nice to meet you."

It had been a natural movement, one I had seen hundreds of times in a pressurized space. What a refreshingly normal person. I almost took my glove off to shake his hand, but as I was reaching for the clasps, I realized where I was.

Dogger watched my expression and laughed as he put his glove back on. The seal around his forearm looked like it was made of duct tape.

"I came to ask about the oxygen tanks," I said. "There was a JPL-390 you purchased a few weeks ago. It's old. Far older than the colony. It has cultural value. Was it the mine you bought it from?"

Dogger pulled out his phone and scrolled through a file. He said, "No, I think that was a cement factory that sold it to us. We buy a lot of scrap from them. What did you think of the initiation? Make you want to join the Fellowship?"

"No, that was the most horrible thing I ever saw. Why would anyone ever do that?"

"You must feel the Earth hunger," he said. "It will slowly grow in your brain, clawing at your mind until you go crazy."

"I think it's the radiation that causes the psychosis, and getting inflated like a balloon seems like a poor solution for Earth hunger."

"You would have to try it to understand. You feel so much more at home here once you've experienced the planet on its own terms. People in the camp almost never complain of recurrent Earth hunger requiring a second treatment."

"You have a lot of oxygen here. Where did you get those other tanks?" I said.

"Oh, we get those from all over. The price of oxygen has fallen dramatically over the last few weeks, so I'm getting as much as I can. We've got about a decade and a half stored up now."

"Do you mind showing me the receipts?"

Turning off his phone and looking up, he said, "Why? We don't steal here."

"No, I wasn't implying that. I don't think those sales were registered," I said.

"I'm not sure why those plutocrats in Promise think they can make rules that apply to everyone else, but I have no interest in making trouble for my business partners."

"Could I just see the receipts for a minute?"

He transmitted, "Jason, can you come escort this man off the mesa?"

I apologized and backed away. This didn't seem like the kind of place to expect people to act reasonable or civil, so I hustled down the path. I did not want to find out who Jason was.

When I was forty feet away, I looked back and saw Dogger on the phone with someone. I wondered who he was calling after our conversation.

The path to the crawler was easy to follow since it was well-worn into the dust. I even recognized a rock that was shaped like a cricket.

I found Dogger's statement about not stealing to be less sincere after I found my crawler was missing. The tracks in the dust led a hundred yards away to a collection of tents next to a table with three men in hardsuits playing cards.

My negotiation tactic consisted of sneaking into the crawler and driving off before anyone noticed. It worked rather well.

As I left the mesa, I was unsure where to go, so I drove a mile north and got ready to sleep for the night.

CHAPTER 10: CONFIDENTIALITY

When the Mars Planning Committee had to decide how to structure healthcare on Mars, they had a lot of models to choose from. In the United States alone, they had over a dozen models to look at. There was the VA, fee for service, HMO, pre-Obamacare, post-Obamacare, Massachusetts, individually owned insurance, insurance through employers, the federally run Indian Health Service, and many more.

The model the planning committee eventually chose was tribally-owned Indian Health Service healthcare. Using this model, they created the aptly named Promise Health Corporation. The funding for the corporation came from property tax, but the corporation itself was not a part of the government. Its shareholders consisted exclusively of the entire population of Promise.

This led to an interesting dynamic where shareholders voted for a board that oversaw a corporation whose customers were all the shareholders. Most health systems talk about trying to keep their patients happy, but few had as strong an incentive as the Promise Health Corporation.

Paranoid of satellites, I had parked my crawler under the overhang of a boulder. The sun was setting, and all my lights were off. I had managed to clean the vomit out of my helmet.

I knew thousands of tons of oxygen were being sold to the Fellowship of Mars without being reported. I knew someone was desperate to kill me. Time to figure this out. I made a list of possibilities for the excess oxygen:

1. Companies could be selling reserve oxygen but not reporting it to MARS.

    Companies always complained about having capital tied up in oxygen they would never use. Random audits didn't include pumping out the tanks to see if they were full of rocks. Selling the oxygen to the Fellowship of Mars would keep the sale from being reported by the recipient.

2. Someone could be producing extra oxygen.

    The greenhouses could be more productive than we knew. We followed the numbers closely, but there could be hidden grain and oxygen. But what would be the point?

Oxygenators were simple technology, and someone could have built several large ones and kept them running for the last year. They took so much power that they shouldn't be profitable. Maybe someone had found a way to make geothermal power work, but why keep it a secret and sell the oxygen to the Fellowship?

Some industrial processes release oxygen. Sodium chlorate produces oxygen when heated, but where could they have found so much of it? I doubted the existence of any large deposits.

3. Something could be using less oxygen than we realized.

People were the main consumers of oxygen. There could be fewer of them than we knew, or they could be smaller or less active than we assumed.

There were a few farm animals, mostly chickens. Similar to people, there could be fewer of them.

An industrial process could be using less oxygen than reported. While several processes used oxygen, the only one that used it on this scale was the bioreactor. It was basically a large compost heap. There could be a cheaper way to make fertilizer, but why hide it?

111

The mine's involvement seemed to limit the source of all this extra oxygen. I could go there and confirm my suspicions, but that did not seem safe.

By itself, my phone couldn't make a call this far from Promise, but it could use the crawler's satellite connection. I decided to call Darnell and turned my phone on. It had been returned in the mail a few days ago, but I was leaving it off due to fear of being tracked.

The phone rang for a minute, then, "Hello, this is Darnell."

"Hi, Darnell. I—"

Darnell cut in, "Where in the world have you been? You left yesterday morning on an audit, and no one has heard from you since. Not even Ryan knew where you were."

"Wasn't I in the news?"

"What for? Have you done something stupid?" he said.

"I was at the warehouse the ship hit yesterday. Hasn't anyone been looking for me?" I asked.

"Don't be stupid. No one had been in that warehouse for a week. I heard Bruce talking about how lucky everyone had been."

"I had fobbed in twenty minutes before the ship hit it."

"Sure. Did you at least get the audit done?"

"No, but I found fifteen thousand tons of unaccounted oxygen," I said.

There was silence on the phone for a minute, then he said, "You're joking, right?"

"No, I'm not. It's all in the Fellowship of Mars camp. They say the price of oxygen has dropped recently, and they've been buying it by the tank load," I said.

More silence.

"Come back to the office. We will talk about this when you get here. I don't know what to think about the ship and the warehouse, but I know you wouldn't lie about oxygen," Darnell said.

When I hung up, I didn't know if I agreed with Darnell about coming into the office, but I didn't have a better plan. It was a little scary to think the FBI had gotten altered fob records from the warehouse. Maybe I should just pull up to their office, run inside, and refuse to leave.

It was dark, but the crawler had bright headlights. I was fifteen minutes into my drive when my phone rang. An acidic female voice was on the other end.

"How much oxygen did you see?" It was Mrs. Lance. She did not do small talk.

"I think there is about—" I started.

"I said, how much did you *see*," she said, stressing the last word.

"I counted twelve thousand one hundred fifty tons if the gauges were all accurate," I said.

"Don't come anywhere near Promise. Don't pay for anything. Keep your crawler's radio off. Turn your phone off. Don't worry about satellites. They're not tracking you. In five days, come back to the office." *Click*. The call was over.

That was unexpected. She hadn't sounded pleased, but she rarely did. At least she was taking things seriously. I decided to do as she recommended. She seemed to have some idea what was going on, and she traveled in the higher circles of Promise.

I still hoped to confirm my suspicions before returning to the office, but I would need a computer for that. Unsure of how I would find one, I pulled the crawler behind a boulder so sunrise wouldn't wake me up, and I went to sleep.

In the morning, shivers ran through my body. It was -70 degrees Fahrenheit outside, but the crawler was well-insulated, and the heater should have been able to keep up.

I turned up the heater on my hardsuit and did my best to rub my arms together. When I still felt cold at a hardsuit temperature of eighty degrees Fahrenheit, I knew I was in trouble. I was lightheaded and felt like standing would make me pass out.

It wasn't until I tried to move that the pain in my leg changed. It was no longer the sharp pain of eroded skin but had become a deep burn.

I drove slowly on my way to The Hospital and only hit two

boulders. No serious damage was done to the crawler, but I wondered how much Father Gray would charge me for it.

Officially, the hospital was named Promise Health Regional Hospital, but since there was only one hospital on the planet, everyone just called it The Hospital.

When I got to the emergency room door, I just fell out of the crawler and hoped someone would come to get me. From the efficiency of the two men with the stretcher, this didn't appear to be an unusual way of getting into the building.

In the emergency room, I had the disconcerting experience of not waiting. That's the universal sign in medicine that someone is dangerously ill.

They had me out of my hardsuit in minutes. My leg was a hot, swollen, red mess. Vital signs were taken, and an IV started. They took blood from more locations than seemed necessary and brought me up to the floor.

By the middle of the day, a young man from the registration department came to do my paperwork. The Hospital had strict confidentiality rules, and I had them add every extra layer of anonymity they could.

I didn't have to worry about billing since all services at The Hospital were free. They didn't even charge for the air.

For most of the day, I was too ill and drugged to do anything besides lie there, but by the evening, I was able to focus well enough to use the computer attached to the arm of the bed.

I couldn't access the oxygen ledger or any other work files from here, but I could surf the web and read the news.

Darnell was right. None of the stories about the ship crashing into the warehouse mentioned me. My bank had to be involved if they hid the oxygen charge from the investigators. I was definitely going to close my account when this was all done.

Looking through the other news, I couldn't find anything suspicious. Narrowing my search to the mine, all I could find were a couple of stories about them opening up a new claim north of their current area. They had brought in three hundred new employees for the expansion.

I didn't dare check my email or contact anyone I knew. My pursuers likely couldn't track such things, but I wasn't taking any chances.

In the morning, I felt much better due to the real bed and my leg being almost the right color. The doctor rounded and told me I would be discharged the next day on oral antibiotics for my cellulitis.

When the registration clerk came through with the paperwork, he also brought me a parking bill. The actual parking was free since Mars was 90 percent parking lot, but they had plugged in the crawler to charge it.

"There's a charge for parking?" I said.

"Yes, it's not medical, so it's not covered. It's only half a pound. I don't think you'll need a payment plan for that," he said.

"I forgot my fob," I said and felt bad about the lie.

"That's fine. We have all your information. We'll just bill your bank directly."

"When will the charge go through?"

"Once I finish my rounds."

"You can't bill me."

"Frugal? You signed permission last night. I've got to move on. Have a nice day."

I tried to stand up and follow him out the door but was attached to the IV pole, a cardiac monitor, and two strange compression things on my legs.

Once I detached myself from all the hardware, I couldn't find the clerk, so I went to the nurse's station instead. They were not happy when I declared I was leaving. They stressed how dangerous it was to leave without a plan. When I insisted, an intern was found who could prescribe me the oral antibiotics.

I considered not picking them up from the pharmacy, but the vivid description from the nurse was convincing. The whole time I waited in line, I was wondering how many patients the clerk had to see before he got back to his desk.

Medications in hand, I limped to the parking lot and started driving the crawler away without any safety checks. The Hospital was located along the southern wall of the valley near its eastern end, so I drove east along the same road I had taken to the Fellowship camp.

Time for a decision. Turning north, I could try to take a look at the bioreactor. Without going in, I couldn't tell if it was running, but maybe I could count vehicles coming and going, though I didn't have any baseline to compare it to. Or, turning south, I could flee into the wilderness.

What made up my mind was when I turned a corner and saw two crawlers. One drove up besides the other for about thirty seconds before swerving away. Looking for someone? Me? I didn't want to find out and went the other way. I was getting out of Promise as fast as I could.

Having left the valley, I decided to take a risk. Ten miles south towards the Fellowship camp, I turned on my phone and dialed Jamie from water accounting.

"Jamie, I just spoke to Mrs. Lance. Can you tell me if beer sales changed at the vending store near the mine after the last fleet from Earth arrived?" I said. Hopefully, mentioning Mrs. Lance would limit questions.

"I heard Darnell say you were off doing audits near the mine. I'll have to look at the ledger. Give me a minute," she said.

About three minutes of small talk later, she said, "I found what you wanted. Fluid sales were up after the fleet's arrival. Do you want specifics?"

"Yes, I was thinking they would have been flat," I said.

"They are up 12.8 percent."

I smiled and said, "Tell Mrs. Lance we had this conversation, and I know what's going on. I tried to avoid coming to Promise but ended up in The Hospital. I'll see her at the office in three days."

As the battery came out of my phone, I did the math. A gold mine with six hundred employees expands its operation by three hundred people, and beer sales only increase by 12.8 percent? Everything fit together. I just needed to live for three more days.

CHAPTER 11: CRAZY SIMEON POST

Mars is cold. On average, negative eighty-one degrees Fahrenheit. Luckily, it's easy to stay warm due to the very thin atmosphere. Heat from a vehicle is lost mainly in two ways: convective and radiative.

The thin atmosphere reduces convective heat loss by over 90 percent since there's 99 percent less stuff convecting. For radiative heat loss, things are even better. The near void allows multi-layer insulation (like satellites have) to function. It has an R-value of over ten thousand. Compare that to the R-19 fiberglass insulation in a wall on Earth. The difference is profound.

While the west exit of the valley of Eshcol led directly onto the wide flat plain of the Elysium Rise, the east exit I had used led me deep into the tall peaks of the Tartarus Montes. I turned north to avoid anyone trying to find me on the southern road; this direction would eventually take me to the Elysium Rise.

There were enough former floodplains between the peaks to prevent any serious difficulties for most of the trip. I made a winding course around individual mountains until I came to the last shallow riverbed. It narrowed to a rocky, half-mile obstacle course. An hour later, I made it through the steep slopes and was out on the Elysium Rise. I had driven over a hundred miles but was only fifty miles from where I had started.

This was a desolate area, like most of Mars. There were no signs of human civilization here besides me and my crawler.

I considered waiting here for the next three days and binge-watching seasons of cheap TV. But I had no food or water. I wouldn't die without them, but it would be unpleasant.

The crawler had a range of 450 miles, and it had been fully charged when I left The Hospital. Tracing out a route to the ruins of Plymouth, it looked like I could make it there in only another 270 miles. Crazy Simeon Post was not the only thing out there; several solar charging stations and emergency ration caches also existed. Ryan had done an audit on an oxygen cache last year and confirmed that everything was still in working order. They were maintained by a small supply company with a contract paid for by the Promise Emergency Fund.

The terrain was flat and smooth, so I was able to keep a pace of thirty miles per hour. When the sun began to set, I slowed to fifteen miles per hour. My headlights were good, but my chest kept tightening at the thought of how alone I was. It was miles to the only pocket of civilization on the whole planet. I slept at 3 am. Normally, I would have stopped earlier, but the hunger and isolation kept me moving.

When the sun rose, I was thirsty enough not to notice being hungry. Every compartment in the crawler was checked three times before I started driving again. There were no forgotten water bottles. I would have even settled for cleaning supplies.

According to my GPS, the crawler was six hours from my destination. My path led me between a gap in the Cerberus Fossae, then south of the gold mine.

I felt much better once the road between Promise and the mine was well behind me.

As Plymouth got closer, I could choose to go directly through rough terrain along the foothills of the Tartarus Montes or swing thirty miles north and stay on the Elysium Rise proper. Being thirsty and hungry, I decided to travel straight there.

I found the area impassable due to a series of steep slopes that marked the edge of an old volcanic flow. I had to backtrack for twenty miles to go around them. Along the way, the crawler started flashing an insufficient-range warning.

My thirst was starting to cause mild delirium, and I almost continued driving despite the flashing red warning. Instead, a review of options on my GPS showed only one known location was within range: Simeon Post's house.

After dealing with the Fellowship of Mars, I was not looking forward to any more crazy, but I had few options. The only other thing I could do besides starve was to call the emergency services. Would I be at the bottom of a ship-sized crater when they found me?

My urgent craving for water made me wonder if Simeon craved Earth. For most people, the Earth hunger gets worse every year. If this were true for Simeon, then by now it must be a constant toothache.

Confidence in the tolerability of Mars had been low after the colonists of Plymouth abandoned Mars. When Simeon later came on a science mission and then refused to leave, it had made Mars seem more hospitable. His decade on the planet before Promise was founded was part of the reason the founding was even attempted.

I arrived at his house well after my battery gauge read zero miles. The top speed of the crawler had dwindled to ten miles per hour.

The structure was in the "early-Earth" style, characterized by a Quonset hut-esque metal frame that had been covered in several feet of Mars regolith. The building had an airlock on both ends. The road past the eastern one was well packed by tire tracks. His house was a bit of a tourist attraction.

In my hardsuit, I walked to the inner door of the airlock and tried my short-range radio. No reply. I pounded on the door with my fists. No reply. The controls for this old-style airlock were mechanical, and all the levers had been sawn off flush with the control panel. The airlock on the other side of the building was welded shut.

I was starving and barely able to stand due to my dehydration. I kicked the first airlock as hard as I could. About two minutes later, a face appeared through the small round window.

His Syrian facial features were still visible through the piles of wrinkles. Even his wrinkles had wrinkles. He did hold the record for the longest time on Mars, though the construction of his house should have prevented radiation damage to his skin.

I pointed to the airlock, and he just shook his head.

Miming the doors opening, I smiled and waved. He shook his head.

I put my hands together in a begging motion. He shook his head and left the window.

It was an hour before he came back to the window. He seemed surprised to see me still waiting there. I tried to convey the urgency of me coming through the door, but he just shook his head and left again.

Returning to the crawler, I felt my heart race. Either from desperation or dehydration, I didn't know. The battery on the crawler was showing as 0 percent. It still had enough energy to keep the lights on, but I wasn't sure the radio could make an emergency call with so little power.

I knew Simeon couldn't understand how desperate my situation was. How often had a tourist acted the same way as me? I needed him to know that without help, I was going to die.

The crawler moved slowly, but I was able to line it up so that its door was as close as possible to the airlock but still able to open. Then I flushed out all the air in the crawler and replaced it with pure oxygen. Without any internet access to look up the correct procedure, I dropped the cabin pressure by 15 percent every fifteen minutes until it was at about 10 percent of normal.

Crawling out of my hardsuit, I waited. Simeon's face did not reappear. I considered my clothes and took off everything besides my underwear.

I was starving, dehydrated, and in the lowest survivable oxygen pressure. I longed for Simeon's face to show up. I also dreaded when he would return. I was sweating even with my dehydration.

His face came back into view, we made eye contact, and I pulled the emergency lever on the crawler's door. The cabin depressurized, and the door flung open with an explosive force. I half-jumped, half-fell out of the crawler. I had never been outside on Mars before. It tasted saltier than I expected.

Unconsciousness found me before any of the unpleasantness started. I awoke in the airlock with both doors closed. I could feel the pressure rising. The vomit on my face was solid, either from all the water in it boiling away or from it freezing; I didn't know.

The blindness didn't bother me as much as the ringing in my ears. By the time the airlock was fully pressurized, my vision had returned, and I flopped around trying to get into the building. Never had a metal floor looked so nice.

He helped me as much as he could, and in a short time, I was wrapped in a blanket and lying on the only cot in the room. He asked about what had brought me here, and my answer was water. It took him a minute to realize I was being literal, and he brought me a cup.

The water improved my condition so much that I felt better than before I jumped out of the crawler. It reminded me of the stories of an early NASA researcher who had eaten his lunch in a cafeteria minutes after a similar experience.

Simeon asked, "How did you end up all the way out here with no food, water, or electricity?"

"I couldn't go back to Promise since someone is trying to kill me, and I was trying to make it to the ruins of Plymouth. I only made it this far," I said.

"Now what? You're stranded here unless you call someone. Sometimes you just have to face the music for what you've done. Unless you're planning on living a simple life like me. Though, you would need to find your own house."

"Why does everyone assume I did something wrong? I just wanted to explain to someone that they shouldn't scrap an antique. Now I've been chased in circles around Promise for the last week."

"Did you ever find them?"

"Who?"

"The person with the antique," he said.

"Oh. Yes. But they were with the Fellowship of Mars, so there wasn't much use."

"Who's that?"

"The Fellowship. They're a cult with radiation dementia who live out in the wastes. Everyone knows about them."

"I don't get out much," he said. "Did they agree not to ruin the antique?"

"The conversation didn't get that far. I ended up running."

"Don't worry too much about it. Mars is only our temporary home. None of us can bring anything with us when we die. I hope you can make peace with the men who want to kill you for protecting the antique. To repay with justice is good, but to repay with mercy is better."

The day was spent with me curled in a ball, being glad to be fed, watered, and pressurized. Simeon stood in a corner with his eyes shut. When night came, sleeping arrangements were him on the cot and me on the floor with the one blanket.

After a few hours, Simeon asked me, "Trouble sleeping?"

"My greatest fear on Mars has always been to die of exposure on the surface. I might be less worried about that now. I'm not sure why."

"You've told me your story. I think you're at your best when solving something. Being on the surface for you is now part of a puzzle you had to solve. It's like the time the emergency structure depressurized on you. You didn't have a second panic attack. Instead, you set about solving your new problem."

In the morning, I continued to greatly appreciate the food, water, and air. Simeon continued to mostly stand in the corner. The room was rather bare. The only furniture was the cot, several crates, and a crucifix in the corner where he spent his time standing.

The crates were old emergency supplies from Plymouth. Simeon told me they were considered jetsam based on the history of Plymouth. It was unclear how much legal weight his argument had, but no one had ever come out to dispute it with him.

Tomorrow was supposed to be the day I went back to the office, but the crawler wasn't charged, and Simeon lived on only four hundred watts of power. Not enough to charge the crawler.

Mrs. Lance would have to be called in the morning. If it was safe at that point for me to drive to the office, then it should be safe to make a phone call.

I knew where the oxygen had come from and why, but I didn't know how Mrs. Lance was involved or what she was doing about it.

When I asked Simeon if he was okay with me making the call tomorrow despite the safety concerns, he replied, "My only desire for you is that you serve God with all your heart and your neighbor as yourself."

I took that as permission.

Simeon didn't have a radio; his rare communication was done from an antenna relay a mile away. My hardsuit was still in the crawler, so Simeon had to don his and go drag mine into the airlock. Once I had mine, I went and plugged the crawler into his solar panel. It wouldn't be enough to drive far, but by tomorrow, I should be able to make a call.

CHAPTER 12: MRS. LANCE

Robert Soto was no longer a normal man who was sick but a sick man with normal days. Somehow that made things better.

He had founded Bob's Cement when he was thirty-two. His was the first company to construct a factory in the Forge, though few people remembered that now. Other cement companies had started since then, and he was glad for it. He loved Promise and wanted to see its future secure before the prostate cancer finally consumed him.

When the next day came, I got into the crawler and called Mrs. Lance. She was abrupt as always.

"Hi, Mrs. Lance, this is—" I said.

"You shouldn't be calling. What time will you be arriving?"

"I'm stranded out by Plymouth. At Simeon Post's house."

"Great. Leave your phone on, I'll call you back," she said with sarcasm and hung up.

Five minutes later, my phone rang.

"Hello," I said.

"They will pick you up in four hours. Don't start negotiating with them." *Click.*

I wasn't quite sure what to make of that, but I went back inside the house for my four-hour wait. When my ride arrived, it was a large-wheeled crawler like the ones the mine used to map out gold deposits.

When I put on my hardsuit and was about to leave, I asked Simeon the question that had been nagging at me for a while, "Simeon, why are you here?"

"I got distracted easily on Earth. Here, the Earth hunger reminds me I'm not home. Jesus doesn't care what planet I'm on, but I was too attached to Earth."

Once outside, the five miners let me into the crawler. I wasn't sure if they were rescuing me or kidnapping me. It quickly became clear they didn't know either. We talked little on the drive.

Our trip was only 175 miles since we could use the west entrance to the valley. The miner's crawler traveled much faster than mine, and we were at the MARS office in a little over four and a half hours. A few hours before sunset.

The miners were large and unshaven, but they were not the most intimidating people to climb out of the four crawlers now parked in the pressurized lot.

Four men in business suits with gun-shaped lumps under their jackets got out of a slick black crawler. They made a point of frowning at everyone.

The president of Bob's Cement stepped out of a different crawler alone and used a cane to walk to the door. I recognized him from my meeting right after I had found the JPL-390.

The last crawler was a rental and contained two people who had their hardsuit sun visors down.

We were what everyone had been waiting for, and soon everyone began to move to the doors.

Once inside, we walked to our smaller conference room. In it, Mrs. Lance sat alone. When she saw me, she motioned for me to sit next to her.

I could see why she had picked the smaller conference room. Only four more people could comfortably fit in it. Four miners, two business suits, and one visored hardsuit waited in the hall. Mr. Soto was the last to enter. All the chairs were taken, so he kicked one of the men in a business suit out of his. With the seven of us in the room, things were tight.

Mrs. Lance began, "You idiots are going to destroy this city.

Attempted murder to cover up actuarial data. Couldn't you at least stick to normal crime?"

Mr. Soto's eyebrows raised at the mention of murder. It looked the same as when I had surprised him by mentioning the JPL-390.

Mr. Soto opened his mouth to speak, but the man in the suit who was standing started first. "What are you talking about? You should be glad that we're talking instead of just shooting you. If we don't like what you say, don't think we won't."

Mrs. Lance made a point of not looking at the man speaking but instead focused on the other man in a suit. "Jason, every FBI agent in Promise already knows the full story. If you don't promise that your trigger-happy friend spends every day cleaning toilets until a ship can take him back to Earth, I will walk out of this room right now."

"Yeah right, you—" the standing man started but was interrupted by the seated man.

"Fred, go wait in the crawler," he said, then added, "Go!" when the man was slow to move.

Once he was out of the room, Mr. Soto asked, "If the FBI knows, why are we here?"

Mrs. Lance's smile broadened into a wide grin. "Good record-keeping, of course. Here's the deal. Every record you changed is corrected. Every company involved issues a full and public confession when the time comes. And no one complains about paying the Emergency Response Fund tax."

"How is that to our benefit? We don't know what companies actually hired imaginary employees. It was talked about as an option, but no one said they were going to do it," Mr. Soto said.

"What you get is time. The FBI has no obligation to report ongoing investigations. If you cooperate, then we will keep looking for more involved companies. At the FBI's request, I will delay making public that MARS discovered massive fraud. If you are lucky, I will find twenty more companies to split the tax with, and you won't go bankrupt."

She continued, "The FBI also says that frequently if a company cooperates with a large civil fine, they won't be criminally investigated. But you will need to give up whoever ordered the ship to fall on one of my accountants."

Jason said, "Why are you here instead of the FBI?"

Mrs. Lance said, "They don't allow anonymous people at their meetings, so not as many people would have responded to the invitation."

Jason said, "It wasn't my team who did the ship, but I know who it was. If we make a deal, I don't want just knowing about it to put me in jail."

"You did more than just *know*," Mrs. Lance said.

"Okay, I canceled a crawler reservation and asked a company to re-file some forms. There is not much illegal about that," Jason said.

The miner said, "My men only went looking around for him with an excavator."

Mrs. Lance replied, "You are incredibly lucky they didn't find him or cause an accident. I know what their orders were."

Mr. Soto said, "I knew nothing of the murder attempt, nor do I approve of it. I only tried to get him a free hotel stay so I would have enough time to move the oxygen, but he never responded. I do not regret hiding Promise's decreasing population. Once it is widely known, the colony will die. Right now, Promise is a pyramid scheme, and pyramid schemes only last as long as the truth is hidden. Promise needs time to grow."

Mrs. Lance said, "It's been forty years. That's a long time. You know that better than anyone. We failed at building a sustainable city. We need to admit it. Until we do, we can't fix it. All you've done is prevent people from addressing the issue for the last several years."

The hardsuit with its visor down said, "This may all be true, but many of my associates can't afford the Emergency Response Fund tax."

Mrs. Lance said, "It won't be as bad as you think. More

companies were in on this than you know. I'm convinced some companies started faking their population numbers without even knowing the rest of you were."

I asked an ill-timed question: "Why didn't you just vent the oxygen into the atmosphere? Why keep it around where it could be found?"

Mr. Soto said, "Oxygen is expensive. We didn't want to lose the money. Though when we could only delay your search by a week, we had to vent some of it."

I said, "And why kill me with the ship? How could that have ever been a secret?"

This time, the miner who I had just driven four hours with answered, "I was told your fob data was being erased. I didn't drop the ship but would have been part of the cleanup. Under the pretense of looking for survivors, we would have found your body and taken it to an incinerator. With a hundred percent oxygen, you would have had no ashes."

Mrs. Lance said, "Back on topic, please. Do you agree to my deal? I will need your confessions within two hours, and they must include the names of all involved companies you know of."

Jason said, "I want assurances directly from the FBI that they won't rope us in with conspiracy charges."

Mrs. Lance pulled sealed letters out of her pocket and

handed each of them one. Jason opened his and read for a minute.

Then he nodded his head and said, "That is thorough. You didn't hear it from me, but Dante Tallino gave the order to drop the ship."

You can learn a lot about people by the swear words they use, and I learned something about everyone at the table with the mention of that name.

Mrs. Lance followed her curse with, "That's my problem, not yours. Make sure your signed confessions arrive on time."

After that, the meeting quickly ended. Once everyone else was gone, I spoke with Mrs. Lance.

I said, "Thank you for finding me a ride home. I appreciate not having to worry about people dropping ships on my head anymore."

"Various leading figures have been hinting for a while at how critically important it is for Promise not to have any population drop. Until you stumbled on the hidden oxygen, I didn't think they had taken it this far," she said.

"How did you know who to invite to the meeting?" I asked.

"I used the last five days to have your coworkers go through all the data in the ledger looking for inconsistencies. We also went through sales data looking for goods that didn't increase when a nearby company hired more workers. Some companies had been so sloppy as to just add population to their payroll without any explanation of where it came from."

"Do you really think people will stop trying to kill me?"

"Jason will attempt to play both sides. He gave up Dante but will also report to Dante every word of this meeting within the hour. When he learns that the FBI has been briefed, there will be no reason to kill you anymore. Also, he won't want to give the FBI an excuse for an arrest," she said.

"Excuse? Don't they have enough evidence already?" I said.

"It's not as simple as that. Dante doesn't actually live on Mars. He owns many businesses here and visits often, but he lives in his Deimos mansion. That moon base flies a Liberian flag out of convenience. The FBI can go there and arrest him based on the concept of universal jurisdiction, but they will need stronger evidence than Jason's word."

"What's wrong with Jason's word?" I said.

"He has been involved in several court cases where his testimony was proven false. He was even convicted of perjury once."

With our conversation finished, I headed to bed. I left my hand on my no-radiation plaque for a full minute before lying down. It was nice to be home.

CHAPTER 13: NORMAL

Humans first had evidence of geothermal energy on Mars with the discovery of the underground lake at the southern pole. This energy was limited on most of the planet, but Promise was built between the fissures of the Cerberus Fossae, the only volcanically active region remaining on Mars.

In the right spots, there was enough heat to keep the aquifer liquid, but at only 130 degrees Fahrenheit, classic geothermal power plants wouldn't function. The efficiency of a geothermal system is exquisitely tied to water temperature.

The water was safe for drinking and plentiful. It was also used to heat the greenhouses since their glass roofs were expensive to insulate.

I woke up in my own bed on a planet that no longer contained anonymous men trying to kill me. Life was good. I showered and went to my desk. Ryan was at his desk, and I told him, "It's nice for things to be back to normal."

"Normal?" he said. "I'm relieved you're back, but you broke the planet."

"We just cleaned up the census data. What's the problem?"

"One of our city's most vocal billionaires has charted a transport to return to Earth outside the normal transit window. The news says it's related to the recent ship crash, but they don't know the details of the FBI investigation."

Preparing my desk for the workday, I lined up my notebook and keyboard.

I said, "Will that really matter for the colony?"

He continued, "Yes, he owns dozens of companies here. It's unclear what will happen to them. Also, once the news of the fake population numbers breaks, don't look at your 401(k). I expect the Mars index to drop thirty percent. Promise has always been a city going through rapid growth—a land of opportunity and wealth. That story changes with a decreasing population."

That morning, everyone in the office stopped by to see how I was doing. It felt good to have so many people care. Everyone had a comment on the FBI investigation.

Benny commented that at least the per-capita production numbers would look better now that the census data would show 302,253 people instead of 305,124.

Jamie was more pessimistic. "We still rely too much on

outside funding. Workers come poor, accumulate wealth, then bring that wealth back to Earth when they retire. Without constant outside investment, Promise won't grow."

Ryan said, "Mrs. Lance has been giving us special projects combing through data trying to find more population anomalies."

Even Bruce came by to see me. He said, "I see you made it home. Stopping the satellite companies from selling your location data worked like I thought it would. I do have bad news, though. They found the technician who had programmed the ship to crash land on you."

"How is that bad news?" I asked.

"He lives at Exit House."

Exit House was the closest thing Mars had to a jail. All serious crimes lead to exile, but since fleets only left every two years, Exit House held criminals until they could be shipped back to Earth. It only had beds for a few dozen people.

Even people convicted of felonies rarely got sent to Exit House. It was expensive to house people, and they did society more good working than sitting in a jail cell. Home monitoring was heavily utilized.

"I still don't think that's bad news. How did he drop the ship on me if he was in Exit House?" I said.

"It's bad news because he's the kind of criminal who won't

turn on Dante. He was in Exit House related to a rather nasty beating he gave a fellow dock worker. His file attributes this to explosive anger problems, but I think it was in retaliation for reporting contraband. He had access to the computer system since he was only listed as a physical threat," Bruce said.

"At least he can be charged," I said.

"Yes. I'll put together a great case for the DA, but he will likely be getting a long enough sentence for his other crime that it won't matter. Dealing with Dante will be more important," Bruce said.

"Why don't you just go arrest him?" I said.

"The only evidence we have is the word of a known perjurer. To even fly up to the moon, Deimos, I will need solid evidence of wrongdoing. Luckily, he owns several companies down here. Evidence linking any of them to a crime would be enough to hold him. I'm sure I'll find something before the Mars supply fleet arrives."

"What does the Mars supply fleet have to do with anything?" I asked.

"The ship he's chartered is coming to Mars with the supply fleet. We think he plans to leave immediately for Earth once it arrives and is refueled. If he takes it to a country on Earth without extradition treaties, we will likely never be able to arrest him. Don't worry—four weeks will be plenty of time.

He's unlikely to start ordering hits on people who exposed his fraud until after he is on Earth."

Once Bruce left, Jane came in and said, "At least Promise made it longer than Plymouth and New Johannesburg."

New Johannesburg had been the first attempt at a colony on Mars. That is where we learned you couldn't do planetary geology from space. Assumptions about the similarities of Mars and Earth geology had been very wrong. The "Diverse geologic conditions" at the landing site turned out to be a two-inch sheen draped over a monotonous block of basalt. Test ice-wells produced as much black dust as desired but no water. The location had been picked by a twenty-six-nation committee, and changing it would have required sixteen legislators, seven dictators, two monarchs, and one religious leader to agree. In the end, countries found it easier to withdraw funding than change the location.

Once everyone had been through my cubicle, things settled down. Ryan said it would be futile to work on the oxygen ledger today, and I agreed. Within a couple of weeks, a dozen companies would be filing amended forms. Until we had those, there was no point in working.

Watching the news, Ryan and I saw various theories about why the billionaire, Dante Tallino, would want to crash the ship into a warehouse. None of the theories were close to correct. Some programs didn't think his abruptly leaving Mars had anything to do with the accident.

Other news stories reviewed the history of Promise and its legal foundation.

Promise was often treated as a territory of the United States; though, technically, it was just a collection of pressure vessels flying the American flag.

When it was founded, funding had come from a diverse set of interests. Launch service providers trying to drive demand, government research teams wanting easy access to Mars, upper-class retirees looking for an exotic place to die, speculators planning to claim large tracts of land, bitcoin billionaires evading taxes, libertarians hoping to avoid government overreach, small countries building acclaim, and entrepreneurs who thought they could make money off everyone else.

The news reiterated the story of how most of the first wave failed, and then the second wave learned from their mistakes and thrived.

Darnell walked in while we were in front of the TV.

"Does anyone work around here, or are you both imaginary employees like all the other companies have?" he said.

He didn't like my excuses. For some reason, he blamed me for not working and not Ryan.

"If you have time to lean, you have time to sort out an oxygen anomaly," Darnell said, misquoting the McDonald's founder.

He continued, "Ryan, you've got that fruit warehouse that's giving you a problem. Take your lazy friend here and go figure it out."

"It's the bananas," I said.

"It's not the bananas," Ryan said, rolling his eyes.

"You're both fired if your report calls the bananas self-depreciating," Darnell said and then left.

Ryan started to fill me in on the puzzle, but I jumped in. "Are the bananas packed close together? Did they place the bananas in a sealed container? Is the plastic being warmed by the light and releasing ethylene?"

"It's not the bananas," Ryan said.

"It's a fruit warehouse, and you're missing oxygen. Of course it's the ripening fruit," I said.

"Just shut up and let me explain what's going on. There's extra oxygen, not missing oxygen," he said. "There are five warehouses that are used for holding fruit prior to sale. In four of the warehouses, as the fruit ripens, the oxygen level drops as expected."

"Could the fruits be photosynthesizing?" I asked.

"Stop interrupting. Picked fruit doesn't really do that. It's dark in there anyways," he said.

He continued, "In this warehouse, oxygen levels are normal, then the fruit is dropped off, and oxygen levels rise for a few days, then start to decrease. The oxygen level ends up slightly above where it was when the fruit was dropped off."

"Then what happens?" I asked.

"The fruit is removed, and the oxygen concentration doesn't change," he said.

"What have you checked so far? Do you think someone is using the warehouse to store stolen oxygen, then retrieving it later?"

"I don't think there is any intentional human involvement. It was the warehouse workers that first noticed the extra oxygen and let us know. Plus, the security footage looks good," he said. "They do use hydrogen peroxide to wash down the warehouse and fruit crates, but I checked the concentration. It's only three percent. Not enough to supply the oxygen even with a complete conversion."

"Windows or lights in the warehouse?" I asked. "Remember that time the light fixtures in the cannery were all filled with water and grew algae. Instead of cleaning them out, they started selling them as oxygenating decorations."

"I remember. No windows besides the airlock, and the lights do turn off correctly. I checked."

"Any other chemicals stored there? Concentrated hydrogen

peroxide or sodium chlorate for someone starting a paper-making business?"

"No, I checked for anything as obvious as that," he said.

"There could be something stopping the fruit from making ethylene. Without it, they wouldn't consume as much oxygen while they ripen."

"I don't think so. The higher oxygen content should increase ripening, and CO_2 levels aren't out of the ordinary."

I asked, "What was that building built for? Do they have any emergency rebreathers in there?"

"It was built for fruit, but initially, they intended it to be a ripening room. Designed with tight temperature control, good airflow, and the ability to add ethylene as desired. They don't use it as a ripening room now since they don't need to transport the fruit far and just vine ripen everything."

"And rebreathers?"

"None. No potassium superoxide," he said and stood. "You want to start heading over there to take a look?"

"No way," I said. "Does the building have its own power?"

"Yes, a kilowatt or so of solar panels to concentrate CO_2 if they need it to slow down fruit ripening. Are you paranoid about leaving the building again?"

"No, but that building is a safety hazard. Did you do a full gas analysis on it?"

"I didn't see the need. This doesn't look like fraud, and the amount of oxygen is small enough not to change anyone's oxygen reserve calculation," he said.

"When a building has its own power, people often don't realize when something is using more power than expected since no one is sending them a bill for it," I said.

His face was showing a glimmer of realization. He said, "You don't think—"

"I'll bet you a hundred pounds," I said. "The only reason the building hasn't exploded is the pressure release valve is probably in the ceiling where the hydrogen will naturally concentrate."

"No deal. I learned my lesson about betting against you. What makes you so sure, though?"

"The slow ramp-up in oxygen that then stops. You said they wash the place down with three-percent hydrogen peroxide. There's not enough oxygen in the hydrogen peroxide to raise the oxygen levels, but there is enough in the water it's dissolved in," I said.

"We still have to go. We can't just guess at the cause and call it good enough. If we analyze the air before stepping in, we should be safe."

"How long's the drive? Should we take sample cups or the analyzer?"

"I hate taking it, but we should bring the analyzer," he said.

For simple oxygen, CO_2, and nitrogen checks, we had handheld meters. For other gasses, MARS had a high-accuracy gas analyzer that calculated concentrations down to parts per billion. It was battery-powered but heavy enough it took two people to move. If it was a short drive, we would take glass sample cups to run on the analyzer back in the office. If it was a long drive, we would take the analyzer to avoid two trips. We all hated the analyzer.

We collected our things, then grabbed the analyzer from the table by the west wall. As we carried it and complained loudly, we passed the receptionist's desk.

Jane noticed us and said, "I can help you carry that out after work hours if you want. That way, two accountants don't have to go. I would go now, but I have to cover the phones."

She was like that, always willing to help even if it meant taking time after work.

"No, thank you. We've got it. Darnell told us to stop sitting around and watching the news," I said.

We made it to the door when Craig passed us and looked at Ryan, saying, "You figure out your extra oxygen puzzle?"

He replied, "Didn't you hear? All the extra oxygen is from missing people. The warehouse only pretends to have zero people. It really has negative two."

He didn't find that funny.

We got our hardsuits on and carried the analyzer to the transit line. We wouldn't need a crawler today since the warehouse was close enough to a terminal.

When we got the analyzer to the warehouse, we just turned it on and put it in the airlock. The readout was visible through the window. Hydrogen content of 3.317928372 percent. Why would anyone ever need that many significant figures? How much weight did obtaining that accuracy add?

It was more hydrogen than I liked but below the 4 percent required to explode. We were able to enter the building safely and look around.

Now that he knew what he was looking for, Ryan quickly found the source of the oxygen. There was a drain in the floor with a sump pump that pushed the drained-water slurry to the tank by the far wall. Removing the grate and pulling the pump up, it was clear from the corrosion the pump was not operational.

After unplugging the pump, we returned home to write our reports and email the warehouse's owner. It would have been a pleasant trip if the analyzer hadn't been so heavy.

Back in the office, Jane congratulated us and let Darnell know we were back. She made us tell her all the details of our trip. She seemed fascinated by how we had solved it.

Soon after getting back to our desks, Darnell came into the room and asked, "You find the source of the extra oxygen?"

I said, "Electrolysis. The water came from when they would wash out the room with a hydrogen-peroxide solution. The hydrogen peroxide had corroded the metal casing around the sump pump, causing it to short out. The building was powered by its own solar array, so no one noticed the constant power draw."

I continued, "Prior to bringing the fruit into the warehouse, the workers would clean out the room, letting the water run down the drain. The water in the drain would cause the sump pump to try to turn on. Electrolysis would then remove the water instead of the normal pumping action. As the water electrolyzed, it would slowly raise the oxygen content of the room, only stopping when it ran out of water."

Darnell looked appropriately impressed, and I continued, "Then the normal ripening of the fruit would drop the oxygen content until the fruit was removed. When more fruit was brought in, the process would start all over again."

Darnell said, "I'm glad you guys got that one out of the way. These next few months are going to be busy. Not only are we going to have to add fifteen thousand tons of oxygen to the ledger, but there's a rumor we might take over the census and part of the fob records."

"I hope that doesn't happen. We have enough to keep track of already," I said.

The rest of the workday was spent writing our report. As the day ended, we got ready to go to Mahoney's Irish Pub. Jamie and Benny weren't coming today, but Jane said she didn't have anything better to do so would tag along.

CHAPTER 14: BROKEN

The first wave of colonists to land on Promise came on 205 ships, each loaded with 100 tons of cargo. They brought with them supplies to set up steel and cement industries, among a hundred other projects.

Cement took precedence over food since a person only eats a ton of food in a year but needs ten times that amount of cement to have a functioning city.

Mahoney's was lively but not crowded. Everyone from work sat at a table and chatted. Lina had come today, and Ryan was walking her around, introducing her to all the people he knew, which seemed to be everyone.

After about an hour, I noticed a man with a cane at the bar drinking alone.

I was intrigued by the thought of talking to Mr. Soto. I went over and stood next to him, watching the blue Martian sunset through the thick glass windows. "Sorry about all the hassle you had back there," he said.

"I believed it when you said you weren't involved with dropping that ship on me. If I had known the emails and calls about a free week in the hotel were real, I would have taken you up on it. The JPL-390 was yours, wasn't it?" I said.

He took a sip of his beer, and his eyebrows narrowed like he was deciding if he wanted to answer.

He said, "I bought it back when we were preparing for the initial Mars transfer fleet that founded Promise. It was in orbit of Mars at the time. Half of the oxygen and all the food in that first two years was brought in and not manufactured on-site. We could have done more in-situ utilization, but all our focus was on getting the cement factory up and running."

I sat down and asked, "Those must have been interesting times, not knowing if a colony could fend for itself. What was it like trying to recreate an industry from scratch? How much did you have to ship in?"

"Shipping a cement factory was nothing new. Almost all cement factories on Earth are manufactured in one place and then shipped to another. A complete cement line capable of producing four thousand metric tons per day has a shipping weight of about three thousand eight hundred tons," he said.

He handed me the drink menu and continued, "That's a lot of weight to ship to Mars, but I didn't have to send all of it. When I designed this cement line, there were several parts it didn't need. I left out the dust-containment systems. Not a problem on Mars."

I said, "Leaving the dust-containment systems behind couldn't have saved you much weight."

"Depends on what you include in dust containment. The cyclone preheater is a dust-confinement and thermal-efficiency device. It's by far the largest thing at a cement plant. My system got rid of it and replaced it with a preheater kiln that brings the material's temperature up to nineteen hundred degrees Fahrenheit. It's an uninsulated, stainless-steel tube that dumps its product into the main kiln. The primary kiln is similar but is made from tungsten, so it can be heated to thirty-six hundred degrees Fahrenheit."

"Tungsten sounds expensive," I said.

"It costs more than steel," he said. "But compared to the price of shipping from Earth, it was not too bad."

I ordered my drink as he continued, "The system turns twenty-four hours a day but only makes cement twelve hours a day. The thermal cycling of day and night is a pain, but not having to deal with refractory bricks is convenient. I also didn't ship a lot of the silos but made them on-site with cement we produced."

"The whole setup is powered by concentrated solar?" I asked.

He said, "Yes, the solar reflectors heat the kilns. When limestone has been cooked, the product is called clinker. It comes out at twenty-four hundred degrees Fahrenheit and needs to be cooled. It's the perfect setup for Stirling engines. Using the waste heat, I power all the electric motors in the plant."

"How did you stay profitable when all the other companies in the first wave failed?" I asked.

"Cement is straightforward. The entire process comes down to heating a rock and then crushing it. To use the cement, all you need is a bucket, a shovel, and some water. Steel, on the other hand, is much more complicated. Even if you make perfect steel, you still need to machine it. It took four attempts before that became profitable."

I sipped on my beer as he continued, "An apartment building for one hundred people on Mars needs about two thousand cubic meters of concrete. That assumes about two hundred feet of living space each, with another two hundred feet for storage and workspace. An Earth building that size wouldn't require so much concrete, but a lot of it is there for radiation shielding, not structure.

"The two thousand cubic meters of concrete would require

about eight hundred tons of cement. My cement factory can produce two thousand tons per day. If all its production went into housing, it could supply enough cement for two hundred and fifty homes per day. If I had sold to residential only, I could have supplied cement for all the apartments in Promise in under four years. But most of my production goes into industrial applications since that is the main consumer of concrete on Mars," Mr. Soto said.

I asked, "Were you able to sell all your product in the beginning?"

"Oh, yes. That first year, I was selling a pound of cement for a tenth of a pound. At that price, no one could justify shipping in steel or other construction materials when concrete would do. I wasn't even able to spare enough cement for my own apartment for eight years. All hundred of us lived bunk-style in one of those rubble-covered Quonset huts they ship from Earth."

"How did your employees feel about that?" I asked.

"They were making quadruple what they could on Earth. There was very little complaining."

Our conversation wandered awhile. We discussed the pros and cons of solar heating, the difficulties of shipping explosives to Mars for the quarry, and the benefits of working in a non-corrosive atmosphere. Eventually, I asked, "Why fake the population numbers? I understand the decreasing population looks bad, but you took a large risk."

"The size of that risk is foremost on my mind. If they don't prove enough of the other conspirators' involvement, I won't be able to pay the fine. But I still stand by my decision. Promise is not ready for this. I sell cement to people who think they can make a profit off other people coming to Mars. Once things begin to slide, this place will fall apart fast."

I said, "We do have exports. Gold, gems, programming. Those make up for our imports."

"If people didn't retire to Earth, we could just make it. But when someone goes home, they take years of earnings with them. We don't have enough exports to keep up."

I said, "How do we fix it?"

"When the price of goods on Promise comes down to similar prices as Earth, then we will be a mature colony. Right now, the price of goods is propped up by continuous investments. We need a gentle coming down off that money, not a sudden collapse like we are facing."

As the conversation wound down, I went back to my coworkers at the table. I felt he was wrong; I had seen the statistics. A person on Mars produces more than he consumes. We were sustainable. I told Ryan as much.

He said, "Yes, on average, a person on Mars produces more

than they use, but that is not good enough. If we were to become a mature colony, we would have a much lower labor-participation rate. Two-year-old children don't work very hard, and someone has to take care of them. If we had a sudden influx of children, we would break even on sustainability."

Jane broke in, "Don't worry about a flood of children showing up. It's hard to imagine the colony working harder to discourage families."

I said, "The colony has been trying to encourage children for decades. I'm not sure what else they could do."

Jane said, "They are only interested in ideas that don't cost money. Think about where you live. The bedroom is three floors below your living room. You have to walk through an office building to use the toilet. I can't imagine taking care of a child like that. If you moved, you would need a new job since half your paycheck is in the form of housing."

"What could they do to fix it?" I asked.

Ryan said, "The same thing people interested in families have been saying for decades. We need to remove the restrictions on having entire apartments underground. If you built them into the side of a hill, you could still have great natural light without any radiation exposure. This split-level living works if you're single but makes parenthood impossible."

"Wouldn't more people leave with such claustrophobic housing?" I asked.

Lina said, "Have you ever been to the shopping district? It's all underground, but it's one of the nicest parts of the colony. I'm too old for kids, but that doesn't mean I don't support the idea."

Jane added, "On average, people stay ten years on Mars. Have you seen the data for women of reproductive age? It's four years. A lot of those women wanted families, but it's just impossible here."

I said, "Why is it different for men and women?"

Ryan leaned back in his chair and said, "The difference is women have limited time to have children. A man can have children at any age. Fertility decreases past forty for men, but plenty of sixty-year-olds have fathered children. If a man spends twenty years on Mars and then returns to Earth, he hasn't given up on having a family. If a woman spends twenty years on Mars, she can easily find herself past reproductive age."

He continued, "And if they stay, why would they have kids here? Earth would be much easier. I like building this colony, but staying forever would be different."

Jane said, "If anyone settles down here, they get to be the grandparents of all Martians. Anything great done on Mars in the future will be done by your descendants. But the colony just isn't set up for families now."

Trying to imitate Ryan's relaxed style, I leaned back in my chair and said, "I don't think housing changes would fix Promise's problems."

Lina said, "This whole city is like one big company dorm. You make proper houses, and women will stay. You make the nursery, and women will come to Mars to have babies."

I said, "Not that again."

Jane wrapped a curl around her finger. She said, "We always bring it up because it would work. You build subsidized housing for women with children that looks like the Windward Resort, and you won't have trouble getting children on this planet."

Ryan said, "That would cost millions of pounds."

Jane said, "If the planning council took this seriously, they could find the money. The fine that Mrs. Lance just arranged would cover the start of the project. Raising children here would still be expensive, but it would be doable on the average salary."

I said, "That would drastically add to expenses. I would have to work years more to be able to retire to Earth."

Jane leaned towards me and said, "Don't you think that would be worth it with the right woman? You wouldn't even need to retire to Earth. If you had kids, you would likely want to stay here to be close to them."

I said, "I don't think I'm likely to meet anyone. No one ever seems interested in me. …Ryan, who is getting free food today, you or me?"

"I think, me," he said.

We bickered about it for a while and decided to split it. Jane seemed irritated and drifted over to the windows, looking at the lights of the city at night. After a while, I went over and joined her. I said, "You okay?"

"I'm fine. It's just, men never seem to be able to tell when I'm interested in them. I feel like I would have to slap them to get their attention. I'm not sure what it takes to get asked out on a date."

I said, "Don't worry. When you're in a room, every man is always paying attention."

She said, "That's sweet. I'm thinking about going home. Will you walk with me?"

She looked very happy that I would walk with her and then confused when I didn't get on the transit line. Why would she think I was going home? I wasn't bored.

Eventually, the evening wound down, and the rest of us left. Walking into my bedroom, I touched the no-radiation plaque while thinking about how hard it would be to have children here.

CHAPTER 15: HUNTING

The 302,253 people of Promise eat 800 million calories per day. Growing wheat in ideal conditions with high CO_2, super-dense planting, and extra sunlight lets you harvest 4 kilograms of grain per square meter every 80 days. That's 18 kilograms of grain per square meter every year. Milling 18 kilograms of grain produces 13 kilograms of flour. Flour has 3,600 calories per kilogram. Putting this all together shows that one acre of growing space feeds 212 people on Promise.

The greenhouses on Promise only have about a third of their floor space dedicated to plants, so 4,277 acres of greenhouse would be needed to feed everyone.

People don't like to eat just wheat, so Promise had about six thousand acres of food-producing greenhouse. That's 12.5 square miles of greenhouse.

Ryan and I were volunteered for Mrs. Lance's quest to find more companies faking their population numbers. A week had gone by, and we both sat at our desks, clicking through thousands of pages of data, trying to think of ways to find the fake numbers.

Ryan said, "What about just going to suspicious companies and counting people walking around."

"That would be possible for a tiny company, but everyone's not always at their desk. What about lipstick sales? Mrs. Lance found a hotel when it 'hired' thirty women, but ibuprofen sales at the stores next to them didn't increase," I said.

"It only works if one company provides a very large portion of a store's business. And lipstick would be redundant to the ibuprofen anyway," Ryan said.

"The vending store near the mine could be a good place to look," I said.

"We've already proved the mine's involvement several times over, and Mrs. Lance has their confession. The low-hanging fruit like that has been found. We need something new and clever."

We sat and thought for a few minutes. I suddenly said, "I got it! Food. We can look at the food numbers."

"That was the first thing everyone thought of, including the companies with the fake employees. They just increased their food purchases to compensate," Ryan said.

I stood. "Yeah, but they have to hide that food somewhere."

Ryan stayed sitting. "They could just put it in one of the communal food depots. Those craters are irregularly shaped, and it would be difficult to tell if the food there was off by a few percentage points."

"That wouldn't work for them. The inputs into and out of those depots are tracked, and if they snuck food in, they wouldn't be able to withdraw it later. They would lose the money. They would have to use a private depot if they wanted to get it back.

"Again, it's hard to look at one of those piles and see how much grain is in one. Our food-audit department mostly relies on the logs from people picking up and dropping off."

I said, "But they are the perfect place to look. The companies report exactly how much grain is in them. If we can show the numbers are wrong, we've got them. Or if we find unregistered grain depots, it's the same outcome."

Still sitting, he said, "Okay, how do you count grain in an irregular crater whose bottom you don't know the shape of?"

"No idea," I said. "Let's go find out."

Shrugging his shoulders and standing up, he said. "Okay, why not? It will be better than sitting here and banging my head against the wall. Which company do we start looking at?"

"Let's look at Great Quality Cleaners. They're a dry-cleaning business with fifteen locations in Promise but only one registered grain depot. Their reports claim their employees went from 73 to 84, four years ago, and then to 96, two years ago."

"Aren't they owned by the billionaire that just fled Mars after dropping a ship on your head?" Ryan asked.

"Yes," I said with a grin.

"Bruce still hasn't found any evidence against Dante's Mars companies that will let him arrest him?" Ryan said.

"Not yet. Bruce continues to be confident as usual, but I don't want to leave his arrest to chance," I said.

As we walked out of the building, Jane asked where we were going.

After we told her, she said, "You want to bet about the outcome? If you find the missing food, I'll buy you dinner. Otherwise, you'll buy me dinner."

"Sure," I said. "Sounds like a deal."

When the crawler pulled up to the grain depot, it was as expected. A crater the size of an average Earth outdoor swimming pool was filled with grain. Where the path came to the edge of the crater, there was a post with a security camera and a sign. The sign identified the site's serial number and listed a phone number to call with any questions.

Records showed it contained 134.6 tons of grain, slightly exceeding the 1.5 tons per person required to avoid the

Emergency Response Fund tax. If it was hiding uneaten food from the missing twenty-three people, then there should be an extra 19.4 tons of grain.

After looking around for a few minutes, we called the number listed on the sign. It was answered by a surly man with a British accent. He was not pleased we were there but couldn't come up with a reason for us not to audit the grain pile.

By the time Bart, the man with the British accent, got to the grain pile, we had a scale, two shovels, and a bucket out.

Bart said, "Why are you here? The logs for this site are all online."

Ryan replied, "Yeah, we know, and they all have your name signed at the bottom. We're just doing an in-person audit."

Meanwhile, I was measuring the diameter of the pile and its height. The pile was much wider than it was tall since grain has a shallow angle of repose, about twenty-seven degrees. A little math using the volume of a cone and the density of wheat showed me the pile held somewhere around 150 tons.

I said, "This pile seems bigger than the records indicate it should be."

Bart said, "That's because the ground rises under the middle of it. All the records are correct. You're just wasting everyone's time."

"You know that filing false paperwork is a crime, right?" I

said. "Just tell us how much extra wheat is here, and we will put in a good word for you with the FBI."

"I ain't done nothing wrong. Feel free to weigh the pile," he said.

And that's exactly what I intended to do as I grabbed a shovel and approached the pile. Ryan didn't move. He pointed out that on Earth, an athletic man can shovel about five tons per hour. Mars has lower gravity, but we were wearing hardsuits. We would likely only get through six tons an hour together. That would mean it would take us over twenty-five hours to get through the pile.

I looked at the grinning Bart and thought it might be worth it. Ryan disagreed. Instead, he took the back end of his shovel and pushed it down into the grain pile until it hit solid dirt. He had me write down height measurements from different points in the pile.

Three pages of geometry later, I swore under my breath. Bart had been right; there was a rise under the center of the grain. More math and my calculations showed the pile was around 130 tons. Nothing was hidden here.

We began to pack up. Bart said, "Satisfied? I told you my numbers were accurate. I was looking forward to you shoveling up the whole pile, though."

"Funny," I said.

Bart said, "That wasn't funny. You want to hear a joke?"

"No."

As Ryan and I finished packing up our stuff, I was not in the mood for jokes. This depot may be above board, but I knew they had extra food somewhere. Who hires twenty-three new people but doesn't increase the number of store locations?

We circled the depot a few times as we drove away, looking for any tracks leading away in suspicious directions.

"Why do people always put those depots in small craters anyways?" Ryan said. "Wouldn't a pile on flat ground work just as well?"

"It would, but people like borders around the things they own, and the edge of a crater acts as a sort of nominal fence," I said.

"They could have their hidden pile of wheat anywhere on the planet. It will be impossible to find," Ryan said.

"Maybe we can follow Bart? He could lead us to it."

"Unlikely, now that he knows we are looking. We should just find another lead to pursue."

Back home, I ordered Jane a gift card for a meal for one person at a local Japanese restaurant. That should make her happy. Then I went to my room, touched my no-radiation plaque, and climbed into bed. I still hadn't come up with a way to find the missing wheat.

CHAPTER 16: RUBBER

Natural rubber is made from the sap of the rubber tree, Hevea brasiliensis. One acre of trees produces about one ton of rubber per year.

To harvest the rubber, a spiral knife cut is made into the bark of the tree, and then the white latex sap drips out. Every three days, another 1.5-millimeter-thick strip of bark has to be cut away. This is traditionally a labor-intensive process requiring one person for every six acres. The Chinese developed robotic technology in the early twenties that allowed the process to become much more efficient. On Mars, the technology was heavily utilized.

A single tree can be tapped for thirty years, after which it is harvested for lumber. On Mars, wooden objects are prized for their rarity, and nothing says wealth quite like solid wood furniture.

I continued to think of ways to prove the dry cleaners were faking their employee numbers. Ryan shot down every one of my plans with ease. I was still sitting at my computer offering a series of bad ideas when Darnell walked in.

He said, "We have a confession that lists several companies as co-conspirators. One term of the deal was we don't admit we were tipped off. I need you and Ryan to find an excuse to go to the Hu Rubber Arborary. Once there, you need to just happen across proof they are faking their employee numbers."

"How many people have they added over the last few years?" I asked.

"None."

"None?"

"Yes, the tip says they've been increasing automation and reducing their actual payroll for the last four years."

Once he left, Ryan and I formed a plan. He thought we could just fake a random audit. I thought it would be better to look into an oxygen abnormality so we would have a reason to poke around for a while.

In the end, we decided to look into a slight oxygen rise that happened once a week. It was almost certainly related to fewer employees being in the building on weekends, but it would give us an excuse.

On the way out of the office, we saw Jane. She was wearing a low-cut dress and high heels. She said, "You lost your bet. How about that dinner tonight?"

I said, "I didn't forget. You should be getting a gift card in the mail this afternoon. I think you'll like it."

She looked confused for a minute, then her face firmed.

She said, "I'm coming with you two today. The phones are slow, and I want some adventure on Mars. Darnell won't mind."

The trip to the arborary was uneventful, but once inside, I found it was the most pleasant greenhouse I had ever walked into. The trees were laid out in neat rows whose branches met in the middle, creating long arched paths. The ceilings had to be tall to accommodate the rubber trees, and the arched boughs provided the impression of a basilica.

The foreman was welcoming and invited us to look where we wanted, only requesting that we didn't get in the way of the robots.

We walked around for an hour, enjoying the space. The only thing ruining the experience was the strong odor.

Ryan said, "We could compare last year's rubber production to this year's and see if they are making relatively more oxygen."

I said, "Even with the same rubber production, the trees may be bigger. Maybe we should try to find a break room and see if there are labeled cubbies."

"Better yet, we should check softsuit-filter sales at a nearby store. See if employees have been trying to block out the stench," Ryan said.

Jane said, "You both are ridiculous. Give me a minute."

She walked over to an employee reattaching a robot's tire. After they spoke for a minute, they both walked over to a little office.

When Jane got back to us, she handed Ryan a shift schedule.

"Here you go," she said. "I think this is what you're looking for."

"How did you get that?" I asked.

"I told him we needed a shift schedule to account for oxygen fluctuations. Apparently, this employee wasn't in on the secret because he just gave it to me," Jane said.

Walking away with the list in hand, Ryan asked, "Are all rubber plantations this pleasant?"

I said, "On Mars, yes. But they have been home to some of the worst crimes in history. Congo was particularly bad."

Jane said, "Do you think when we go through the schedule, we will find the proof we need?"

"I don't think so. That would be too easy," Ryan said.

It was that easy. Both Ryan and I were stunned they had just handed Jane the proof of their fraud.

I said, "Maybe they didn't think it was a big deal. Like there would be no penalty if they got caught."

"I guess they could have convinced themselves they wouldn't have to pay any penalties. Technically, they were meeting their backup resource requirements," Ryan said.

"Still, they just handed it to us," I said.

"Being assertive is working for me. But still, that employee couldn't have known," Jane said.

"I wonder if this trick could work anywhere else. If companies haven't told their employees they are faking the numbers on the reports, we could just go ask supervisors for schedules," Ryan said.

We stopped by seven more companies that day and got schedules from four. Three of them showed far fewer employees than the official reports.

Our smugness came down a couple of notches when we visited a branch of Great Quality Cleaners near the shopping district. The man behind the desk had heartily agreed to give us a schedule. He told us it would only take a few minutes for the manager to bring it down. It took three hours and twelve excuses before we realized it was never coming.

As we walked out the door, the man at the desk said, "Are

you sure you don't want to wait a little longer? I'm sure the manager will be here any minute."

We left without replying. It had been the third time he had said that.

Still, Darnell was quite impressed by our results from the day. He said, "I'll have everyone working on this go out and try it at a dozen companies tomorrow. We should soon have enough to go public."

I asked, "How did all these numbers get so far off to start with? Wouldn't someone have noticed the empty seats on the ships coming to Mars?"

Darnell said, "We've been looking into that. Companies often charter entire ships and split the room between passengers and cargo. Some of the flights seem to have only had cargo, even though they had declared them as passenger flights. Since the companies were the ones unloading them, no one else noticed."

CHAPTER 17: LEGACY

On Earth, many cultures have struggled to preserve corpses. Promise had the opposite problem. With temperatures well below freezing and no soil microbes, a body laid on the surface would last a millennium unless it was near the relatively warm equator. Some people preferred this. On the peak of a nearby mountain, rows of bodies watched the years pass in tombs of stone.

But most people wanted their bodies shipped back to Earth. Like Joseph returning to the promised land. The planning council required all employment contracts to offer this option, and many people took it.

Cremated remains had similar options. Ashes were scattered on Mars and Earth in about equal measure.

Two days later, I had piles of shift schedules on my desk. Ryan had noticed an odd trend. Many of the schedules collected during the beginning of the day clearly proved a company had been faking their population numbers. None of the schedules collected at the end of the day showed the same thing.

"I guess they realized what we were doing," Ryan said.

"We still caught several of them. It should be a crime to file incorrect reports like that," I said.

"It is. You know that."

"I know. I mean *more* illegal. These numbers are used to plan out everything, including how many emergency resources we need. Accuracy saves lives," I said.

"Stop complaining. We know a few of these later reports are inaccurate. But they only had a few hours to make the fakes. Let's see if we can find the counterfeit ones."

Looking through the records was tedious. It was mostly just names and shifts.

A few hours later, Ryan said, "I give up. How am I supposed to know if Ana Stanton works eight to five at a mill or if John Saville works noon to nine at a strawberry farm?"

I grinned and laid a trap. "How could anyone know? I'm getting bored here. I'll bet you fifty pounds that at least one of those two records is a fake. We'll go to the listed employer and ask to speak with John, then we'll do the same with Ana."

John Saville had been working at a wheat farm when I met him a couple of months ago.

I swore under my breath when we went to the strawberry farm and immediately crossed paths with John in the field. We talked to him and found out he had recently switched jobs.

But at least my £50 was safe after the mill couldn't produce any information about an employee named Ana Stanton.

Back in the office, I found a letter on my desk addressed to me. Mr. Soto had died.

There weren't many funerals on Mars. Accidents were rare, and retirees were rarer. Mr. Soto was the first person I knew who'd passed away here.

I had talked to him several times since that night in the bar. He had enjoyed telling stories about the early days of colonization as much as I had liked listening.

Still, I was a little surprised to receive an invitation. He didn't have the biggest company on Mars, but he did have the oldest. This was going to be a large affair.

The invitation said the ceremony would take place at a quarry that his cement factory owned.

When I arrived, I learned that Mr. Soto had chosen to be laid to rest on a block of stone surrounded by a ten-foot stone wall. The mausoleum had no roof.

I had once heard him say that he loved looking up at the stars since they were the same on Mars and Earth. It had helped him feel at home.

The ceremony itself was in the quarry warehouse. Mr. Soto was Catholic, so Father Gray officiated. It was a classic Catholic funeral service, and afterwards, many speeches were given.

Mrs. Lance's speech was uncharacteristically long. She talked about Robert's steadfast dedication to Promise, how he had been the first leader to make the colony work. The end of her speech was something only a few people in the audience could understand.

She said, "When I last saw him, Robert talked to me about beauty and how there was beauty in truth. He told me how being able to die without any secrets was one of the best gifts he had been given."

After the ceremony, I avoided mingling. I hadn't spoken with Father Gray since texting him that I had left his dented crawler hundreds of miles from Promise. It was getting repaired, but I was sure I didn't want to know what the final rental bill was going to be.

Walking in my hardsuit to the transit line, I reflected on how comfortable I was outside. The landscape here was flat and open, though the nearby solar reflectors gave the sensation of being on the edge of some strange forest. I lay on the ground and looked up. It was reassuring to know the stars were the same here, though I didn't know enough constellations to confirm it.

"Jack Maddox lying on the ground. That's how I found you last time."

I winced. It was Father Gray.

"I was just remembering how Mister Soto used to say he was comforted by the stars. I decided to try looking at them for a while," I said.

"Was that where you were looking when you ran my crawler into a boulder?" he said.

"That was more of a medical issue. I'm sorry I abandoned your crawler in the wastes."

"Don't worry. The repair shop assures me it will be in perfect condition when they are done with it. No expense is being spared," he said.

I winced again and stood up. "I'm glad to hear that. Wouldn't want them sparing any expense."

"Mrs. Lance says you were the one responsible for finding the population manipulations. You did a good thing for Promise," he said.

"To be honest, I didn't do it for Promise. In the beginning, I was just trying to look for an antique, and in the end, I was running for my life," I said.

"All the same, thank you. The colony will go through growing pains now, but the truth is where strength is found."

"Don't you mean shrinking pains? I still don't really

understand why the population drop is such a big deal. How much real difference is there between a small gain and a small drop?" I said.

There was a knee-high rock a few feet from us, and Father Gray walked over to it and sat.

"Promise has always depended on outside investment. In the beginning, it was a hundred percent of the economy. Without outside investment, we would still be a barren waste. Now we are less dependent on it, or we would be if a fifth of our population didn't leave for Earth every two years," Father Gray said.

"Why does that matter?"

"We replace the people who leave with an almost equal number of new immigrants, but it's an unstable treadmill. If the immigrants ever stop coming, our population will rapidly decline. This makes us very susceptible to an economic downturn."

"You think people won't come because they saw the population dropping?" I said.

He shook his head and said, "I think no one will pay for their ticket. The programmer crowd will always pay their own way, but everyone else comes for a job. On Earth, when someone loses their job, they often get stuck in whatever city they are in. They then look for a new job and try to make things work. On Mars, if you can't afford to be here, you get shipped back to Earth."

"So, you're saying that if the population drops, companies will lay off workers. Those workers will leave for Earth and not be replaced. The drop in population will then cause other businesses to be less profitable, and they will also ship in fewer workers, leading to further population drop."

"Yes. It's like a normal economic downturn, but this is a place where investors don't have a reason to believe things will always recover. When New York City has a recession, everyone assumes there will still be a city there in twenty years. On Promise, it is easy for investors to see us going the way of the last two colonies," he said.

I said, "If public perception becomes that Promise is shrinking, investment will dry up, and the balance will tilt towards a contracting economy.

"And that contraction will scare away any remaining investment, finishing the collapse.

"We are going to publish the true population numbers soon. What can we do to stop a collapse?"

"Why do you care? You're leaving," he said.

"Just because I'm leaving doesn't mean I don't care. When I'm back on Earth, my life will be enriched just knowing that Promise is still here."

He sat in silence for a while and then said, "Do you really want to know how the collapse can be avoided?"

"Yes."

"Stay. When we stop losing twenty percent of our population every two years, Promise will be stable."

I didn't answer as I sat and thought.

He said, "The other option is change."

"What change?"

"It doesn't really matter as long as the investors think it will cause Promise to grow again."

"Wouldn't it be better if the change actually fixed the colony's underlying problems? Made things sustainable?"

"Being sustainable on Mars is not about resource sustainability. We achieved that years ago. If all access to Earth was cut off, we would survive. It would be tough for a while, but we have enough industry to make it work. No, sustainability on Mars means livability. Can you convince people to invest their whole lives here and not just visit for a short adventure?"

"How do you do that?"

"I don't know how to convince other people any more than I know how to convince you. I'm just a priest. Fixing the planet isn't my job."

"Aren't you on the planning council? It is your job."

"Even so, I don't have an answer."

We sat and talked for a while more. Eventually, the conversation wrapped back around to Mr. Soto and his burial.

I asked, "What do you want when you die?"

"We've been having an ongoing discussion about that at the church. Some advocate for putting the bodies in the bioreactor so they can be recycled into the soil that feeds all life in the colony. But that doesn't sit well with Catholic theology. We believe in the resurrection of the body on the last day. Others in the church advocate burying the bodies with a heater, so they decompose just like they do on Earth."

He stood up and walked towards the transit line. I joined him.

He continued, "I personally favor burial in a simple casket six feet underground. It's cold enough you will never decompose, but there is plenty of land here for graveyards."

We made it to the transit line and parted ways. I felt good about the encounter until a few days later when I received the final bill for the crawler. Apparently, his gratitude for what I had done did not extend to offering me any discount. Truly, no expense had been spared.

CHAPTER 18: CONSEQUENCES

When planning for Promise, the committee looked at prior NASA data. An astronaut needed 0.84 kilograms of oxygen, 2.42 kilograms of water, 1.77 kilograms of food, and 4.56 kilograms of other supplies per day. So, a 100-ton cargo ship from Earth could provide food, water, spare parts, and oxygen for 25 people for a year.

With a well that reaches the aquifer, the supply ship could skip the water and focus on the food, oxygen, and spare parts. This would allow it to support 34 people.

Adding oxygenators like the NASA MOXIE would allow the supply ship to only bring food and spare parts, supporting 39 people.

Once farms were built, the supply ships only had to bring spare parts, bringing the number of people supported for a year to 54.

The spare parts were numerous and varied but included motors, wires, laptops, valves, and reagents. All things that need to be replaced over time. About half the spare parts needed were simple, like valves and wires. They tended to be heavy and easy to make. Promise was able to manufacture these on-site about ten years after its founding. A single cargo ship could then supply 109 colonists for a year.

The price to ship a ton to Mars had stabilized at $100,000. Those shipping costs added $92,000 to the otherwise high cost of living on Mars.

While this enormous additional cost of living was the greatest risk to the colony's future, it was also its own solution. New manufacturers had a captive audience and only had to charge just below the shipping price to guarantee a sale until competition arose.

What would have been a $95 AC motor on Earth cost $750 to ship to Mars. Making it for $300 and selling it for $700 provided a healthy profit.

The numbers were even more appealing for heavy industry. On Earth, a forty-ton excavator would only cost you $400,000, but to ship it to Mars would cost $4,000,000. Many of the early factories shipped half the weight from Earth and manufactured the large metal bits on-site.

As time went on, the price of goods steadily dropped. Companies that hadn't quickly recouped their initial investments went bankrupt as they competed against companies whose startup capital costs were only a third of their own.

The types of goods imported from Earth slowly dwindled. Only the most difficult or lightest goods were shipped in. Among them were microchips, medicines, turbines, esoteric chemicals, and rocket engines.

Promise grew and only required a twentieth of the spare parts per person as it had in the beginning. Each cargo ship supported 1,090 colonists for a year. Since fleets arrived every two years, the support part of the fleet consisted of 278 ships.

The atmosphere on Promise was festive. The biennial Mars supply fleet would start arriving by the end of the week, bringing goods people had been waiting two years for.

I hadn't ordered much, just a CPU upgrade for my computer. With a total shipping weight of six ounces, I had only paid $18.75 to get it here. That's £0.38.

What I was more excited about were the orders MARS had made. There was a handheld atmospheric analyzer and another rack of servers.

My desk was covered with oxygen reports from all the companies who had confessed. Mrs. Lance was coordinating with the FBI on going public, so a finished accounting was needed before the Mars supply fleet arrived.

The FBI planned to be present for the disembarkation of every ship, while the planning council would start a planetwide census.

Enough evidence had been collected to get the planning council to act. A third of the council had been proven guilty and were having their arms twisted by Mrs. Lance.

Looking back to where Ryan and Darnell were talking, I said, "It's all working out, but I just wish we could have included one company owned by Dante Tallino. Bruce still doesn't have anything to arrest him with."

Darnell said, "They will be caught once the census is done."

Ryan said, "That won't get him arrested. He will leave hours after the fleet arrives. And his companies won't even get fined. Mrs. Lance is insisting that for the census to be accurate, it has to come with amnesty for incorrect numbers. If we want them to pay, we have to catch them before we go public."

Darnell said, "Why do you dislike them so much?"

I said, "You would feel the same if they dropped a ship on you. And Bruce keeps hinting that Dante isn't someone to let this drop once he is safely back on Earth."

Darnell pointed to the piles of papers on my desk and said, "True, but accurate population data comes first. Once you've finished going through all those reports, you can try to dig something up on Dante's companies."

It took me three days to get through the reports. Ryan was less helpful than usual since he spent half his time texting with Lina. She was signing a four-year contract with her apartment building and wanted Ryan to renew his MARS contract for the same length of time.

Ryan already had two more years on his contract, but Lina felt it was better if the contracts were in sync. The text he showed me said, "That way, we can stay together or split up without external pressures."

By the time the reports were done, I only had two days left before we were going to go public. I had to act fast. I reviewed the outlines of a plan with Ryan.

We were at our desks when I said, "You get crayons and paper while I buy a new phone, then we will visit the cleaners."

"Remind me again why it needs to be in crayon?" Ryan said.

"This needs to be believable. Make sure the letters are all different colors, so it looks like the Fellowship really did write it," I said.

"Okay, I'll post the fliers. But who is going to answer the phone?" he asked.

"Jane said she would do it. She was actually quite excited when I asked her if she wanted to spend the evening with us," I said.

By the end of the day, we were ready. On bulletin boards near all the Great Quality Cleaners were signs written in crayon, stating: *Looking for cheap wheat for the Fellowship, in a hurry, please call.* Then it listed the number for the phone we had just bought.

Ryan and I had spent much of the day visiting different branches of the cleaners, asking to speak to managers. While waiting, we would loudly talk about how the FBI was combing the wastes looking for illicit grain depots.

We hoped the combination of signs and visits would lead to a catch.

That evening, Jane, Ryan, and I waited with the phone. Lina was conspicuously absent, but Ryan didn't mention her all evening.

The phone never rang, but we had a nice time talking about the latest gossip. Mrs. Lance was pushing the planning council to use the money from the upcoming fine to provide subsidized housing for families with children.

Jane was quite excited about this and kept talking about all the features it could have, like domes, playgrounds, and lawns. She asked if I thought it would be nice to live there. I was indifferent. How would either of us ever get one of those apartments? Neither of us had any kids.

The next day, we waited for a call again. It came while we were eating lunch. Jane answered, "Hello, this is Jane. Can I help you?"

It was difficult to hear the reply, but the couple of words I did hear sounded like a British accent.

"Yes, I'm looking to purchase about fifty tons of grain. Can I pay you in peridot?" she said.

More muffled speaking.

"Okay, normal money, then. How soon can I pick it up?"

When we had the location for the meeting, I called Bruce.

He said, "I didn't think your little stunt would work. But now, it should be easy to finish the case. But I didn't figure you would be one to lie about being part of the Fellowship."

"I walked on the surface without a hardsuit, so it's not technically a lie. I meet Fellowship of Mars entry requirements," I said.

Bruce let us drive with him to the location in a large dump truck.

Ryan and I kept our sun visors down when we got close to the location. No need to let anyone recognize us. I was grinning when I saw Bart standing by a pile of grain. He wasn't smug at all once Bruce finished his conversation with him. He had very unpleasant things to say about Ryan and me, but at least he admitted who he was working for. Not that it was entirely necessary.

Back at the office, we hurried through the paperwork. We handed it in with our final reports to Mrs. Lance.

On television, the news broke much like we had expected it to. Surprise and alarm that so much of the colony's data was faked. Dropping stock prices. Statements from the planning council about how this would be avoided in the future, including a census run by MARS. The FBI declared they would be present for every disembarkation for the upcoming Mars supply fleet.

Mrs. Lance was doing interviews, pushing hard for a series of reforms she felt would improve the colony.

Enough companies had been included in the fine that no one declared bankruptcy. A surprising number of companies supported Mrs. Lance's idea of amnesty for those caught in the upcoming census.

Dante was arrested hours before his ship arrived. Bruce said it would take several months to fully put their case together, but they had time now.

Over the next several weeks, things finally settled down, and the news began focusing on what the supply fleet had brought. Just like after all the previous supply fleets, dozens of companies were being founded.

There was a collection of electronic manufacturers, including one for laptops.

Jane's favorite was a company that was going to start cultivating coffee beans to replace the ubiquitous instant coffee.

I was most excited about a jam producer who was going to add blueberry to the flavors they offered. I had gotten a little tired of strawberry.

The economy always boomed around this time in the cycle.

All these new manufactures needed buildings, fixtures, and housing for their employees.

It was also the time for contract negotiations. In the end, Ryan did sign on for four more years. Lina talked about staying on the planet long-term; Ryan wasn't willing to commit to that but also wasn't going to rule it out either.

Mars felt much more like home now than before my adventure. The walls and floors were so safe. My walk outside showed me how pleasant the inside of my apartment was.

Life was back to normal. I just wished I would meet a woman who was interested in me, but life is never perfect. I had my job.

At least I enjoyed my time with my coworkers. Everyone was getting along well. Jane had insisted on talking alone after work today, but I don't think she was upset. Maybe it was something about the dry cleaners.

I loved keeping all my detailed records.

AUTHOR'S NOTE

Thank you for reading my book. I was thrilled to share with you my vision of Mars. The story of Promise was set seventy years from now, but that is likely a pessimistic time frame. I really do think we can start constructing colonies on Mars within our lifetime.

Please consider posting an honest review of this book, as they are the metric that decides my success or failure. I read every review and look forward to your feedback.

If you have any friends who would enjoy this book, then please consider recommending it to them. They value your opinion. The more people we can convince that large scale Mars colonization is possible, the faster we will get there.

There are lots of numbers in this story. I stand by my math for them all. For those interested in where the numbers came from, I have included a list of references. It does not cover every fact in the book but does include the most interesting ones. If you think my science is wrong, feel free to contact me.

I have self-published this book and did not have a large editing budget. Please excuse any typos you found and let me know about them, so I can fix them for future editions.

Arc.True.Author@gmail.com

REFERENCES

Bruce G Bugbee, Frank B Salisbury. Exploring the Limits of Crop Productivity: I. Photosynthetic Efficiency of Wheat in High Irradiance Environments, Plant Physiology, Volume 88, Issue 3, November 1988, Pages 869–878, https://doi.org/10.1104/pp.88.3.869

Francisco J Arias. On the Feasibility for Mining the Hydrogen Peroxide of Mars for Monopropellant Rocket Fuel. Department of Fluid Mechanics, University of Catalonia. EPSC Abstracts. Vol. 13, EPSC-DPS2019-12-2, 2019

Häder DP. On the Way to Mars-Flagellated Algae in Bioregenerative Life Support Systems Under Microgravity Conditions. Front Plant Sci. 2020 Jan 8;10:1621. doi: 10.3389/fpls.2019.01621. PMID: 31969888; PMCID: PMC6960400.

Hofstetter, Wilfried & Wooster, Paul & Crawley, Edward. (2009). Analysis of Human Lunar Outpost Strategies and Architectures. Journal of Spacecraft and Rockets - J SPACECRAFT ROCKET. 46. 419-429. 10.2514/1.36574.

Richard W Bancroft, James E Dunn. Experimental Animal Decompressions to a Near-Vacuum Environment. https://ntrs.nasa.gov/api/citations/19660005052/downloads/19660005052.pdf

Roth EM. Rapid (explosive) decompression emergencies in pressure-suited subjects. NASA CR-1223. NASA Contract Rep NASA CR. 1968 Nov:1-125. PMID: 5305515. https://ntrs.nasa.gov/api/citations/19690004637/downloads/19690004637.pdf

https://nssdc.gsfc.nasa.gov/planetary/factsheet/marsfact.html

Printed in Great Britain
by Amazon

75264766R00123